3

MW00810332

WILDERNESS RECKONING

Caraway's Return

Warren Troy

Joy,

Sometimes we do what
Needs to be done,
AND damn the consequences!

W— T
Willow, AK

PO Box 221974 Anchorage, Alaska 99522-1974
books@publicationconsultants.com—www.publicationconsultants.com

ISBN 978-1-59433-425-2
eBook ISBN 978-1-59433-428-3
Library of Congress Catalog Card Number: 2013955313

Dedicated to my loving and loyal wife, Joyce Hansen Troy,
Without whose language skills, patience and grit,
none of my books would exist.

Manufactured in the United States of America.

Chapter One

Denny Caraway woke up in his log cabin on Lanyard Creek. He had returned to his homestead after being a long time gone, when the grief of losing his wife, Gwen, caused him to move deeper into the Alaska wilderness, removed from everyone and everything he cared about. He had been away for more than a year and a half.

Caraway was a man of exceptionally strong spirit, which enabled him to bear many hardships and misfortunes, yet remain whole. This inner strength had come forth as he struggled to create his first homestead above the head of Long Bay years ago and after his move to Lanyard Creek, living on his second, more remote wilderness home.

But even his determination and grit couldn't keep Denny from succumbing to the dark state of mind that sent him into self-exile when cancer took his wife. His meager, difficult life in hiding, alone with his grief and pain, had wrought changes in the man, changes that made him, in some ways, more like an animal dwelling in the forest than a civilized person.

It was the loyalty of a good friend, discovering him one freezing winter day where he was struggling to survive in a very small old trapper's cabin, that had signaled the time for a return from his seclusion.

Now, after a week, Caraway found that just being back on his homestead hadn't made things good again. His prior contentment in living the homesteading life had been overwhelmed by the depth of his sorrow.

Being back in his snug log cabin, however, did give Denny some solace, and he knew it was the only possible place for him to regain inner peace. Gwen was buried up on the low ridge behind his place. Having her close, even now, was a comfort to him. His self-imposed penance in the deep forest was over. He would give the life he had so loved a chance to work again.

The one thing troubling his mind, which would take a long time, if ever, to leave him, was the guilt Caraway felt, blaming himself for Gwen's death.

Denny had plenty to keep him busy, getting the homestead back in good shape. Deserted for so long, it had been invaded by animals as well as the elements. Caraway hadn't closed the cabin door when he left, and it didn't take long for predatory creatures to make a ruin of the log cabin's interior. It would take some time to fully clean it up and make repairs.

The homesteader also needed to build up a good supply of firewood. Though nearby sources of suitable wood had been depleted over the years he had been harvesting it, there was still plenty of forest to supply him with dead, dry spruce and birch, scattered among the living ones.

Caraway found his snow machine still covered with a heavy canvas tarp in the lean-to behind the old plywood cabin he had lived in before building the log home. He poured a little fuel into the engine from a plastic gas can that had remarkably been left undisturbed. After several pulls on the starter rope, the engine fired right up. So, he had means available to make skidding firewood much easier and for making his first run back to the highway at Salcha, when he was ready to reconnect with people.

Denny had climbed up to the cache and found what was left of the jars of moose meat and salmon. He and Gwen had canned part of the last moose they had taken several winters ago, as well as fish they had caught the summer before she had passed. Almost all the jars were broken, the contents gone bad from freezing in winter then rotting, as the temperatures turned warm. Under normal circumstances, they would have been transferred to the cabin before frigid weather arrived. Still, there were a few unbroken jars of viable meat left. He cleared the ruined food and broken glass from the cache, burying it at a distance from the cabin.

Caraway knew it would be necessary to hunt for a moose soon, though the meat in the undamaged jars would sustain him for a while. Compared to the meager diet he had been surviving on, the canned meat would do fine for now. He had a small amount of dried greens to use in soups and meat stews, gathered where he had been existing and brought back to the homestead.

Denny knew he couldn't live on just meat for very long, but the animals that had raided the cabin left no dry goods intact, save for a few handfuls of dried beans and lentils he had salvaged from the floor and countertop. He could hang on for a few weeks, when it would be necessary to go for much needed supplies. He'd hunt before then. Bringing food back to the homestead would help him feel re-connected to the place.

Denny still had the great love for Alaska he'd known since coming to the north country. It had helped keep him from going under more than once, some beautiful scene or unique moment keeping his life intact after all else had worked to bring him down.

Chapter Two

On the hunt, the woodsman lifted a hand to shade his eyes from the glare of the cold winter sun. While it provided a few hours of light, there was scant warmth emanating from the pale, shining sphere.

Though certain he had seen something slipping through the trees on the far edge of the tundra, it had been too fleeting a glimpse for him to be sure what it was.

Denny had been hunting moose for most of the day, a process he had gone through often since he had begun living in the Alaskan wilderness many years ago. Some years he'd taken more than one moose, or a moose and a spring black bear. One animal was usually plenty of meat for a single person living remote, but he had shared his isolated life for several years with his wife, Gwen, and providing for two had required two moose per year. Alone again, one would suffice.

There it was again, a movement between the birches, but this time he recognized it as a wolf, perhaps one of a pack, in all likelihood hunting in the area. With such competition, he realized any moose nearby would be unavailable to him. Caraway turned and began snowshoeing back to his cabin. He'd try again the next day in a different location.

He hadn't backtracked more than a few minutes, when he heard a loud crashing in the trees off to the right of the tundra he was traversing.

A young bull moose, perhaps three years old, came storming out of the trees, stopping short as it spotted Denny standing a short distance away. It was obviously fleeing from something, and Denny was sure it was running from the wolf he had seen. Caraway had no qualms about taking the moose for himself, knowing every living thing in the bush was in competition for survival. The wolves would have to find another animal.

The old lever action Winchester, the one Gwen had inherited from her dad, came smoothly and naturally up to his shoulder. As soon as the open sights lined up properly on the moose, he touched off a shot. The rifle fired a large caliber bullet, with a heavy load of powder behind it. The heavy recoil was unpleasant, but Denny, concentrating on the target, didn't notice.

The moose's four legs buckled from the impact of the large bullet. It was a perfect heart shot, and the animal fell on its side a moment later, dead.

The rifle's report was very loud, so Denny was surprised to see three wolves come out of the trees onto the edge of the tundra and stand still, looking from the moose to him, and back again. They weren't certain why the moose was lying there, or what the noise had been, but they seemed to sense the man had something to do with it.

Caraway began walking the thirty yards to where the moose lay, which was only a few feet from the wolves. One of them lowered its head, hackles raised, snarling as Denny slowly approached.

Working another round into the rifle's chamber, he calmly told the wolves they would have to find food elsewhere. "The moose is mine, so you need to go now; go on." The "go on" was spoken firmly and a little louder. Two of the wolves turned and slipped away into the trees, but he could see they had stopped nearby and were watching the third wolf, which hadn't moved.

Denny knew this was the lead wolf, and it wasn't going to give up the moose easily. Raising the rifle to his shoulder again, he fired a round very close to the wolf's front feet. The predator jumped straight up, turned in the air, and disappeared into the forest, followed closely by the other two.

Denny got busy with the task of dressing out the bull. Now, he had fresh meat.

Finished with dressing and quartering the moose, Caraway carried a hind quarter on his pack frame to the cabin, before running the snow machine and sled out to his kill. Luckily, the wolves hadn't returned. He was able to haul the rest of the moose in one load, leaving the offal for hungry animals: wolves, foxes, birds, and perhaps even a wolverine.

Later that night, the meat all butchered and stashed away in the cache, he was able to relax, the fireplace blazing, feet up on the table, with a mug of Labrador tea in hand. Looking around the cabin, he was feeling better about being back, the old satisfaction of building a good home and living the remote life slowly slipping back into his heart.

Caraway had the mental strength to keep from falling back into the bad state of mind that had been his lot, after Gwen died. He knew she wouldn't want him to feel so low. With the cabin seeming more homelike again, he was beginning to think he might be all right, back on Lanyard Creek.

Perhaps it was time to head to the highway, where the trail came out at the little community of Salcha. Though he knew only three people there, one of them was the best friend he'd ever had.

He went to bed that night the way he had since returning. The mattress having proven too soft for him after the hard little bed he had been sleeping on, he laid several blankets and his sleeping bag on the floor to sleep on.

The next morning, Denny prepared to ride the winter trail to town, which he hadn't done for a long time. Still, he didn't have to think what to do or take, preparing for a run being second nature to him.

Caraway loaded up the sled with empty gas cans and trail gear, topped up the snow machine's fuel tank, and headed west to the Richardson Highway, towards civilization.

The night before he left, Denny had sat late into the night by the fireplace, in the chair his wife, Gwen, had brought from her parent's old cabin. The crackling fire put his mind into a calm state, and he wandered in and out of the important moments in his life, the high and low points, the happy and sad times.

He turned his thoughts to Charlie Brady, a true friend who had never given up on him, who'd found him where he was hiding from the world and, in truth, had brought him home. Caraway intended to show his appreciation. He wasn't one for great shows of affection, but he knew what he would do.

He didn't drop off to sleep until the wee hours of the morning. As Denny finally fell into a peaceful slumber, he felt as if Gwen was all around him, a comforting feeling.

Caraway understood now why an old homesteading couple who had lived near his first homestead, well before he had arrived there, were so devotedly connected to their home deep in the woods, and why the husband had left after the woman he truly loved had passed away.

What he wondered, however, was why he had never returned home again. Perhaps a good friend had never told the man it was time to come back.

Riding on the familiar trail, Denny found himself filling with life again. Long denied, his emotions came rushing to the surface, and tears rolled from his pale blue eyes.

He saw several moose on the way to Salcha, and a coyote sniffing under a tree. Startled by the noise and movement of the snow machine, the yodel dog ran a dozen yards into the trees, before stopping and turning to watch as Denny rode by, its focus on whatever was beneath the tree now broken.

Caraway was strongly connected to the forest, after dwelling there for so many years. But the connection had become even deeper, after living close to the edge, as he had been over the past year and a half, sometimes barely staying alive. He had struggled to survive the same as any other animal in the woods. Now, he had a different perception of things, a new pair of eyes to see the land in a fuller way, as he traveled along the trail back to civilization.

For no specific reason, Caraway's memory touched on the drowned man whose body he had retrieved from the creek years earlier, and how grateful the grandmother and grown children had been to be able to take him back home. He didn't have strong family ties of his own, having lost his parents as a young man. His grandfather had been his guardian and friend after they passed. He had instilled in Caraway a love for and knowledge of nature.

Denny had never visited the dead man's family, who were Native people, though they had come all the way out the trail, guided by Charlie Brady, several weeks after Denny had brought Henry Pete's body to Salcha. It had been a good experience, sharing time and food with them. Caraway decided it would be right to go see them up in Fairbanks some time.

By mid-afternoon, he reached the Richardson Highway, where the trail came out on the north end of Salcha. The darkness of winter had placed no extra burden on his journey, enhancing it instead.

He rode over to the North Star Cafe, Charlie Brady's place, and parked his snow machine. Denny sat on the Skidoo a minute, setting his mind right. Taking a deep breath, he walked in.

It had been a little over a month since Brady had last seen Caraway, in the deep woods. Charlie didn't know if his visit had done any good; he didn't know if he would ever see his friend again. He had returned to the routines of his life, reluctantly leaving Denny to whatever his destiny might hold. Time slipped by, as it always does, no matter what the demands of the human condition.

Brady had been cooking and was bringing out one of his big, hearty breakfasts to the only customer in the place. As he came through the swinging door to the dining area, Charlie stopped short, causing the toast to slide off the plate.

There, standing inside the front door, was Denny Caraway. He looked the same as Brady had found him in the woods that winter day, very lean, with an overgrown head of hair and bushy beard, his clothes stained and patched, but not wearing the coyote skin hat, now. Caraway still had a distant, hard look in his eyes.

Putting the plate of food on the counter, Brady walked up to Denny and gave him a big bear hug. At first, Caraway tensed up, but he relaxed

9

after a moment. Pushing him gently away, he stuck out his hand and said, "Afternoon, Officer Brady."

Charlie grasped Caraway's hand firmly and responded in kind. "Afternoon, Mr. Caraway. Come for the free meal I offered you?"

"As a matter of fact, I'd appreciate a burger, fries, and some coffee."

"Coming right up."

After taking care of the other customer, who sat with a look of curiosity on his face, watching the interaction, Charlie cooked Denny up a special burger, with lots of extras on it including two bacon slices, an egg, and a split link sausage, with a large pile of fries on the side.

While Charlie cooked, the customer couldn't help stealing glances at the rough-looking man sitting nearby. Finally, Denny turned his gaze on the guy who, after a few seconds of the Caraway stare, dropped his eyes to his plate until his meal was done, then left some money on the table and made a bee-line for the door.

Charlie brought out the massive burger, and Denny put all his attention on eating it, savoring every mouthful. Charlie stood nearby, gently shaking his head. Watching the way Caraway devoured the food, Brady realized how he must be feeling, with the big plate of food in front of him, after such a long time surviving on, if he rightly assumed, meager rations.

Denny had consumed every morsel and was sitting back with a second cup of coffee, feeling quite full. Charlie reluctantly told Denny some unfortunate news.

"I hate telling you this," Charlie said, "but Elliot passed away, a month ago."

Denny paused, the coffee mug halfway to his mouth. His expression didn't change, but Brady thought he saw a flicker of something in Caraway's eyes. The homesteader replied, "Sorry I missed seeing him off."

Charlie nodded. "His grandson, Drew, has been taking care of your old trailer, like Elliot used to, and running your truck occasionally to keep it fresh. In his will, Elliot left Drew his house."

Denny said, "I enjoyed the meal, and Charlie, I won't be wanting cinnamon in my coffee any more. I'll be at my trailer."

As Denny headed for the door, Charlie called out, "Hang on a second, Denny, let me get your Winchester 30-06. I kept it cleaned and oiled while you were gone, but you can take it back with you now."

"No, Charlie, I want you to have it."

Brady started to say something, but Denny put his hand up. "Charlie, if it wasn't for you, I'd still be working hard to survive out there, and who knows if the next winter might not have gotten me. So, you keep the rifle.

I've got Gwen's Model 71 Winchester, and I've come to really appreciate it. Thanks, Charlie."

Denny headed out the door, leaving Charlie to consider how fortunate he was to still have Denny Caraway as a friend.

As he stood there, Charlie said, "Yeah, they broke the mould after that one."

Chapter Three

Leaving the North Star, Denny headed down to the old trailer he had used for a home base when he was in Salcha, ever since buying his homestead. George Levine, the man he had bought the land from, had included the trailer in the deal, and it had proven very useful.

Drew had continued taking care of the trailer and truck after his Grandpa Elliot died. Drew was a solid, reliable person as his grandfather had been, always willing to help out, as most Alaskans would. He was also very capable and had natural mechanical abilities. He had learned to hunt and fish from his granddad, Elliot, as Denny had from his own grandfather, though thousands of miles apart and at different times.

Hearing a snow machine approaching, Drew looked up from where he was sweeping some stray snow from the front stairs. He was amazed and happy to see Denny Caraway on it. He stood there, mouth slightly open, staring at Denny's changed physical appearance.

Caraway finally said, "You'd better close your mouth, Drew, before your tongue gets frostbite."

"Wow, Mr. Caraway, it sure is good to see you. I didn't know if we ever would again, but Grandpa Elliot told me you had some things to straighten out, and you'd be back. I've got a pot of coffee going in the trailer, if you'd like a cup."

"No thanks, Drew, I filled up at Charlie's place. Truth is, I'm tired, and I'd like to stay the night at the trailer, if you wouldn't mind."

"Why would I mind? It's your trailer, after all."

Denny shook his head. "Drew, I turned it over to your grandfather and gave him the deed. Since he's gone, it's yours by all rights. I'm sorry to hear he's gone."

"That's good of you to say, but as for the trailer, it's yours. Grandpa told me to take care of the place and keep your truck running. But the trailer is still yours. He never changed the title to his name. I even renewed the registration a while back."

The young man paused to smile, the look on his face showing obvious pleasure at being able to tell Caraway he had taken care of things for him.

Denny stood looking at Drew, his mind absorbing what the young man had told him. "Your grandfather was a good man, and I can see you take after him. I appreciate everything you've both done, and I owe you. If there is anything I can ever do, let me know, okay?"

"Well, I'd really enjoy going out with you to spend a little time at your homestead. I've always wanted to see it. Never been out that far. I bet it's beautiful country."

Though Caraway really had no desire to have anyone with him on the homestead, he said, "Yeah, we could do that sometime."

The two Alaskans, the old homesteader and the young man, shook hands, and Drew left Denny to his own devices. It didn't take long for Caraway to get settled in and not much more time before he was fast asleep on the couch. He would never admit it, but lean times in the deep bush had taken a toll on him physically. Though still a strong man by most standards, living in the wilderness demanded much of a person, even at the best of times. Perhaps being back now, he could regain his full strength and health.

Morning found Denny still snoozing on the old couch. He hadn't moved since falling asleep. Coming around, he stood and stretched to work out the kinks, which were always there in the morning lately. He moved around the trailer and heated the coffee remaining in the pot. Finding some food in the fridge, he fried some eggs, drank a quick cup of lukewarm coffee, put his shoes back on, and went out to get the truck warmed up. In a few minutes, he began his drive up to Fairbanks. Denny had checked his hiding place in the floor of the closet under the cheap carpeting and found his stash of money still there, making it possible to restock the food and supplies he needed.

It wasn't a long drive, but Denny's mind was full of thoughts about the visit he'd make to the Barker home up on Chena Ridge. He needed to see his former employer, Nathan Barker. He owed Nathan an explanation. Besides their work connection, Denny and he had become close friends. They were two men who shared a love of the Alaskan wilderness. Caraway thought it only right to explain his long absence.

What he didn't know was that Barker had journeyed down to Salcha after Caraway had dropped out of sight. Denny hadn't been in touch with him since Nathan had helped get Gwen back to the homestead to spend her last days. Denny's worried friend had met Charley Brady while making inquiries, and Charlie had told him what little he knew. After learning of Denny's total disappearance, Barker had conducted a search with his plane, to no avail. He and Brady had made contact several more times, but there had been no news, and ultimately Nathan needed to focus on his own life, though he never stopped wondering.

Denny pondered whether or not he should ask Nathan about working for him again. Though his disappearance was something he had to do, he regretted leaving his friends to wonder what had happened to him. If Caraway was to re-establish himself, he needed to make money to live on. He couldn't think of working for anyone other than Barker, if he'd have him. He'd find out soon enough.

As Denny drove north on the Richardson, he continually observed his surroundings, the same way he scanned the forest he lived in, always on the look-out, especially when hunting. It was this deep conditioning that caused him to pull to the side of the road suddenly, while going through a stretch of relatively flat country with stunted black spruces scattered throughout.

Off to his right stood a large, all-white bull caribou, barely thirty yards away. Denny got out of his truck after shutting off the engine. Still, the animal stood facing him, seemingly unafraid.

On impulse, Denny raised both hands high, palms towards the pure white animal. At Caraway's movement, the bull ran in a small circle, two, three, four times, coming to a stop facing the man. He snorted, then lifted his head, crowned by a massive rack of antlers, and moved off into the trees in the gliding motion caribou have.

It seemed to Denny as though it had actually faded away, rather than trotting into the distance. Giving his head a quick shake as if to toss the odd scene from his mind, Caraway climbed back into his truck and continued north.

Soon, he arrived in Fairbanks and headed towards the Chena Ridge area and the Barker house. He didn't think about it, half fearing he might turn around if he did.

The log home was as impressive as the first time he had seen it, with its large log walls, wide front porch, and stairs of split spruce. But his mind was on other things.

Standing directly in front of the house, Caraway took a deep breath and walked up to the front door. As he reached for the large brass knocker, the door opened, and Nathan Barker, not yet aware Denny was there, walked out. He stopped, stunned by the close proximity of this man, his good friend whom he hadn't seen for so long. He ran his eyes up and down Caraway, observing the physical state of him, before grabbing Denny by the arms.

"My God, Denny, where the hell have you been? Lord, it is good to see you. Please, please come in."

Denny was unable to speak for a moment, all his hidden feelings stirring within him, delight at seeing his good friend and remorse for having left without saying good-bye. He waited for Nathan to berate him for disappearing.

But his worries were unnecessary. Nathan was simply glad to see him again, to know he was alive and apparently well, though lean as a rail and a little worse for wear.

Nathan led him by one arm into the living room. Without asking, he poured them both a double of good scotch. Denny didn't object.

"Here's to your safe return, Denny. I've got a lot to talk to you about, but I know I have to give you some time to adjust."

Denny hadn't said a word yet. He sat quietly, listening to Nathan. But, when Barker paused for a moment, he began talking, a flood of words pouring out of him.

Nathan was surprised at first, never having heard Denny talk this much, but he quickly realized living isolated for a long time might do this, even to someone such as Caraway, normally spare with his words. So he quietly sat and listened, as Denny told of his existence and experiences, living as he had been. Denny himself was surprised by the force of his own words, but couldn't stop speaking.

Nathan noted Denny hadn't said anything about Gwen's death, and he didn't plan to ask him.

All of a sudden, Caraway paused in his flow of words, then he said, "I'm sorry Nathan, you deserved to know where I was, instead of being left to wonder."

"No need for apologies, my friend. I don't know what I would have done in your place. The important thing is you're back, and you're all right. I hope you'll let me know if you need anything. Whatever it would take to make things all right for you, consider it done."

Denny was going to ask Nathan about working again, when Caroline came walking into the room, obviously pregnant. Denny forgot what he was going to say. He stood up and just looked at her, at a total loss for words. Caroline looked at him for a moment before saying, "I don't know whether to hug you or slap you, dammit. Where have you been?"

She closed the distance between them and locked her arms around him as best she could.

Caraway stood there, arms at his sides, not knowing what to do. Then, without thinking, the hardened, fearless homesteader put his arms around her very gently. He hadn't felt a woman's touch since Gwen had passed, and Caroline was a dear friend. He took in a deep breath and let out a sigh.

Touched by his reaction, Caroline quietly shed some tears, sensing how this must be for him. Stepping back, she took her sleeve, wiped the tears from her eyes and smiled.

Nathan walked up and put a hand on Caraway's shoulder, saying, "Welcome home, Denny."

Caroline went into the kitchen to fix a meal for the three of them. She had noticed Caraway's physical appearance and felt the need to cook for him. He sat talking to Nathan, but the smells coming from the kitchen were very distracting. At the table, Caroline told him to dig in, and he didn't hesitate, eating with real enthusiasm. Nathan and his daughter gave each other a look, feeling sorry for their friend, but very glad to have him back.

After the meal, Caroline excused herself, needing to lie down and rest.

Denny and Nathan spent the rest of the evening catching up, with Nathan telling Denny about the way his business had grown, expanding into Canada and other locations in the Lower Forty-Eight, mostly in more remote areas where the inevitable process of development wrought its changes. At several points, Denny was obviously a little disturbed by what Nathan was telling him, about the major development projects Barker was involved in. Noticing this, Nathan made it clear to Denny how all his surveying, planning, and designing buildings were oriented towards keeping the land as unchanged as possible.

"I make it a point to create places and spaces to fit into the environment where we're working. I enjoy the challenge of building as unobtrusively as possible, but still creating what the client needs. Though I spend a lot of time at home doing the designing, I first study the place we are dealing with. I often spend a week or more there, getting a feel for the place.

"As a matter of fact, Denny, I've been working on a project of my own, when I find time. I'd like to talk to you about it and get your opinion, but it's late. Why don't we hit the sack. We'll talk in the morning after a good breakfast. I don't suppose you have any objections to some fresh eggs and bacon, maybe caribou sausage?"

"I could manage it, Nathan. The dinner Caroline made was really good. I've eaten a lot of moose, but that roast was extra tasty. Can't remember the last time I had fresh vegetables."

"Well," Nathan said with a smile, "it explains why there weren't any left by the end of the meal, including the mashed potatoes. Don't think I've ever seen anyone eat so much without falling over."

"I definitely feel like falling over now, Nathan, so I'll say good-night."

As he was leaving the room, Nathan suddenly asked Denny if he had ever wanted to go to Africa.

The question gave Caraway pause. He said it was something he'd never considered, even though Africa had always seemed a fascinating place to him. "I usually get all the adventure I need right here at home."

During their conversation, Denny had mentioned to Barker the white caribou bull he had seen and its peculiar behavior. Nathan was curious about the creature.

"I've seen several white animals, Denny. Many native cultures see them as spirit animals and messengers. What puzzles me is there shouldn't be any caribou there at this time."

"Another Alaskan mystery, Nathan. Good night."

Denny walked to the bedroom he was to sleep in. Opening the window, he stood breathing in the fresh, very cold air, until his face felt tight. He shut the window again and got into bed. The mattress was way too soft for him, same as the one at the homestead. As he had done in his cabin, he laid several blankets on the floor. After pulling the comforter over him, Caraway fell into a deep and dreamless sleep.

And so, life for Denny Caraway, with the support of his loyal friends, was beginning to feel worthwhile again. But the homesteader was different after what he'd been through, both emotionally, from the loss of Gwen, and physically, from surviving in the deepest wilderness with the barest of essentials. Those experiences had pared him down to a man whose reactions were even closer to the surface. Always ready to deal with whatever came along, it would now take very little for him to react without hesitation and do whatever he felt a situation demanded. Though the support and love of his friends had begun to smooth out the rough edges, the man's wild streak would always remain.

Chapter Four

After the hearty breakfast he had promised, Nathan asked Denny if he was in a hurry, or did he have time to go on a flight with him.

"I want to show you the place I purchased last summer, rather than merely talk to you about it. We can take the Otter I bought recently. I think you'll enjoy flying in it."

Denny was happy to go with Nathan, pleased that Barker had asked him.

"The place I am going to show you is where I mainly want you to work this coming summer, but let's go see it first."

They hadn't even spoken about Denny working for Nathan again. But now, without any discussion, it was settled. Denny could forget his concerns.

They drove over to the Fairbanks airport where the plane was kept. Denny was impressed. It was like a big brother to the Beaver, with greater passenger and cargo capacity and a more powerful engine. As he expected, the old plane was in perfect shape. He knew Nathan wouldn't have it any other way. They walked around the aircraft, inspecting its condition.

"I could have purchased a more modern plane, but to me, De Havilland aircraft are the epitome of bush planes, though there are some who have argued the point with me. I got the Otter because I wanted a plane that could carry more building supplies or more passengers and their gear. Impressive isn't it? It was made in Nineteen Sixty and has a six hundred horsepower radial engine, but for its weight and size it does surprisingly well on short landing strips and is easy to land with floats on. Well, everything is good; shall we go?"

In a short time, after the preflight checklist was gone through, the two men were winging their way to the remote location where Barker had purchased land on Burl Lake.

Nathan was an accomplished pilot, and Denny was always glad to fly with him. He appreciated the unique view of the terrain that flying at low altitude afforded. Denny stored what he saw in his memory for possible later use.

It took just under an hour to reach Burl Lake, flying northeast from Fairbanks. Nathan tapped Denny on the arm and pointed off to the right.

"Can you see the lake about five miles away?"

"Yes, is it Burl Lake?"

"It is, in all its natural beauty, my friend. Keep watching it as we get closer. Its dimensions will surprise you as we come in."

Nathan was right. For some reason, the lake grew quickly as they flew closer. Caraway figured it must be at least three miles long and two wide. There was heavy forest right up to the shore most of the way around, except for a stretch roughly a hundred yards long on the east side of the lake. It looked as if someone had cleared it for shore front, but Nathan assured him it was natural.

Coming around for a landing, Denny thought he spotted an old relic of a cabin about a quarter mile from the east shore.

Nathan confirmed what he saw, "I believe it must be an old trapper's cabin. I found about half a dozen rusty traps, some old pots, and a lantern. Who knows what happened to the trapper?"

Denny nodded, knowing there were a number of reasons a trapper might no longer inhabit a cabin, most of them unpleasant.

The lake surface was covered with smooth snow. Denny barely felt it as the Otter touched its skis down. Nathan pulled up to the cleared lake shore and shut off the engine.

It was very cold as they stepped from the plane.

Nathan led the way to a spot on the edge of the tree line. There was a small, crude, wooden shelter there, mostly covered with snow.

"This is where I stayed last summer, when I came to inspect the land."

"How much of the lake is yours?"

"From the center of the clear area, half a mile in either direction and into the forest about a hundred yards. I'll have fishing rights for the whole lake. I must admit I had to pull some strings and call in a couple of favors to lock down the section I bought, but I strongly felt this was something I needed to do.

"I plan to build the lodge in the center of the cleared area right up against the tree line. The ground here is great for building, compacted and stable, with no permafrost. I plan on bringing in the logs so I don't have to clear any trees from the forest around the lake. There will be a main lodge building, plus three cabins for the clients, and several outbuildings.

"I want a maximum of three or four clients at a time. They have to be dedicated fishermen, with wilderness experience. I'll select the clients myself and only plan to have a total of twenty-four to twenty-eight clients total per season.

"This lake is full of native fish, and I want to hold the catches to a level that will keep the lake healthy. The main rule will be to keep what you catch. I have never cared for the catch and release system. It can be very hard on the fish. Well, the rest of the details will be worked out as we build. So, what do you think?"

Denny looked all around as Nathan described what would be a wonderful place for avid fishermen. The site had a good feel to it.

"With you doing the designing and building, Nathan, it may well become the best fishing lodge in Alaska."

"Especially with you managing the place for me, yes."

Denny turned and looked Nathan in the eye.

"I know this is something you couldn't have considered, but I think it would be great for all of us. I'd love to be here myself, but my business keeps me on the move."

Denny stood looking out at the lake a while, before answering, "I appreciate the offer, but I'm not really sure what I want to do at this point. I wasn't expecting this. I need some time to think about it."

"I understand, Denny, but I thought of you being here the first time I came, though I didn't even know at the time if I'd ever see you again. I knew you'd love the lake and the country around it. This place is gorgeous in the summer. It's a perfect site for a lodge.

"I plan to have boats with smaller four-stroke engines. Minimal pollution. You'd love it, Denny, and I can't think of a better man to take care of it.

"Oh, Caroline wants to spend time here, too. She isn't going to teach any more and has always loved the wilderness. Chad's leaving after he learned she was pregnant was very hard on her, and being here might help her get over it."

"What kind of man would leave? It is his child, right?"

"Yes, it is, Denny, but he wasn't the man we thought he was, and that's all there is to it. Caroline and I don't talk about it any more. I'd be glad if you were here to keep an eye on her. Give it some thought. You'd be well paid, of course and have whatever you'd need."

"I'll consider it, Nathan. You probably won't be working up here until spring, and I have to get back to my cabin soon, but this is certainly a beautiful place. I can see why you chose it."

Before leaving, Barker told Caraway that he had named the lake and showed him why. Directly behind the site where he would have the lodge built, about fifty yards into the trees, was a very large, old white birch tree. It had a thick trunk with many burls on it, particularly one really massive growth, perhaps five feet in diameter, eight feet up the tree.

"It's magnificent, in a gnarly sort of way, isn't it, Denny?"

"It is, Nathan, one knotty old tree, all right. I can see why you chose the name."

On the flight back, Nathan explained to Denny why he had asked him about Africa.

"I've been to Africa four times. As you know, I've taken a number of fine animals. I'm making one more safari next September, to get another Cape buff and try for a leopard. The spotted cat has eluded me every other safari, though I came awfully close last time around. Unfortunately, a lion showed up. The leopard sprang from the bait tree and disappeared into the underbrush, with the lion in hot pursuit. I was right on the verge of making the shot, but I had to give it up. So, I want to try for a leopard one more time."

"It sounds like an exciting experience. I hope you find what you're looking for."

"I figure the lodge should be completed by early September, Denny, and then I want you to come with me to Africa. I have the whole trip set up with a well-known professional hunter, Jan Vermeulen. I met him in Zimbabwe on my second safari, and we took to each other right away. So, he'll be my professional hunter this time.

"Zimbabwe is a terrific place, so I'm going there again. It would be great to include you. Interested? I'll have everything covered. I would be honored to have you with me. We could call it a belated celebration of your return."

Denny didn't know what to say. This was more than he could have expected and a little overwhelming. It seemed a chance for his life to open up again, a real renewal. Perhaps going to Africa would help Caraway feel complete again. It would be an opportunity to see a different wilderness, at the very least.

At that moment, everything Barker had offered him made perfect sense.

"Nathan, it's yes to everything."

"Yes?"

"Yes, but you know I'm not a trophy hunter, so I'll come along to see Africa and share the adventure with you."

"Perfectly fine by me, but you'll need to have a heavy caliber gun along, just in case, at least a .375 H&H."

"Oh, I think I've got an excellent gun for the safari, no worries."

The two men were cut from the same cloth. They continued talking all the way back to Nathan's home, like two boys scheming together.

As Denny lay in the blankets on the bedroom floor, he drifted off to sleep feeling more alive than he had in a long, long time.

Chapter Five

Denny was in Fairbanks, purchasing needed supplies for himself. A date to start work had been set, and he'd said good-bye to Nathan and Caroline. Though the reunion had been far better than he expected, Denny wanted to return home for the solitude he needed, so his mind could settle down again, after all the interactions he'd just gone through.

Though he didn't consciously acknowledge it, he also needed to have Gwen nearby. He knew she was gone and had no delusions with regard to her passing, but it helped him to know she was resting nearby, on the land they both loved.

Denny was almost through, gathering the dry goods and perishables he needed to be well stocked on his 'stead. Browsing through the store, he found it a little strange to merely reach out and pick up bacon, butter, and coffee, after he'd been without these things for so long. Now, it was almost too easy to have them once again.

Caraway had finished loading the supplies into his truck, when he caught a glimpse of someone he would have preferred never to see again. Almost directly across the parking lane from him was Carlton O'Bannion and another man, in conversation. While visiting with Nathan, Denny learned O'Bannion had spent ninety days in jail, paid a large fine, and lost his hunting guide license, because of the illegal way he ran his guiding service. Denny wasn't surprised at the news, nor did it bother him that O'Bannion had been punished for his low-down ways.

Caraway had worked for O'Bannion four years earlier, hired to build two hunting shacks in the remote area where O'Bannion guided hunters. After the shacks were built, O'Bannion had talked Denny into taking an inept client on a grizzly bear hunt, because his assistant guide had quit suddenly. But the hunt had gone very wrong with the difficult and useless client, almost causing Denny his life.

Carlton had been unable to find another assistant, his hard-nosed, mean-spirited personality well known in the Fairbanks area. Despite the bad hunt, O'Bannion had tried to bully Caraway into continuing to work for him, but Denny stood his ground and wouldn't do it. Furious, the bad-tempered guide had left Caraway marooned in the remote bush, to find his own way back.

But O'Bannion didn't know Caraway well. Denny had simply packed his gear and walked out, despite it being a long trek through country unknown to him. It had taken days to return to civilization.

The season had been a dismal failure for O'Bannion, and that alone had formed a deep-seated grudge against Caraway, who he blamed for the loss of business. But when he was charged with illegal guiding practices, O'Bannion was positive that Caraway and Nathan Barker were responsible and it intensified his anger.

Barker had gone to see O'Bannion after Denny had related the incident to him. A long time Fairbanks resident and an avid hunter, Nathan was familiar with O'Bannion and his unethical ways. Barker had gone to O'Bannion to get the back pay the guide owed Denny, convincing him it was the easiest way to settle things with Caraway.

Full of loathing for the two men, O'Bannion vowed to someday have his revenge.

Though Caraway felt a hot rise of anger at seeing him again, O'Bannion hadn't spotted Denny yet. So Caraway decided not to confront him. He'd had a good, positive visit with Nathan and Caroline and wasn't in the mood to go dark.

But, as he opened the truck door, O'Bannion saw him. The guide said something to his companion and pointed at Denny, and they began walking towards him. Denny stayed where he was and shut the truck door, not wanting to get caught inside the cab.

O'Bannion walked up to within six feet of Caraway, while the other man stepped off to the side a short way and stood watching.

"I was hoping we'd bump into one another sometime, Caraway. I know you and your snooty friend Barker are responsible for the trouble I've had. You two bastards have ruined my life!" O'Bannion's face went beet red after blaming Denny and Nathan for his problems.

Denny didn't react to Carlton's rant except to quietly say, "The only person responsible for your trouble is you, O'Bannion. I haven't forgotten the way you did me, and as far as that goes, I'm glad you got what you deserved."

Caraway spoke quietly but firmly, but inside he had gone cold, waiting for whatever was coming next.

In reaction to Caraway's remarks, O'Bannion yelled something unintelligible and stepped forward, reaching out for Denny's throat. But he came to an instant stop, as if a switch had been flipped off.

In the second it had taken him to reach Denny, Caraway had pulled his old hunting knife, honed to a fine edge and stuck the blade under Carlton's chin, the point slipping a quarter inch into the man's flesh.

The two men stood there unmoving for several seconds, a tiny rivulet of blood beginning to run down the blade of Denny's knife. O'Bannion's partner flinched in reaction to what had happened and slipped his right hand into his coat pocket. The movement wasn't missed by Caraway.

"Tell your friend to take his hand out of his pocket."

Denny put a little more upward pressure on his knife, causing O'Bannion to instantly put his hand up, palm towards the other man, who hesitated, before withdrawing his hand from where it had been wrapped around a small revolver. He stood silently, watching his partner and Caraway, waiting for the scene before him to play out.

"O'Bannion, I'd love nothing more than to end your time, and I don't really care what happens afterwards. But I have plans and don't intend to let you ruin them for me, so back away. Do it!"

The anger in O'Bannion's eyes hadn't diminished, but he knew it was over. The man carefully lifted his chin until the blade was free and stepped back, waving at his friend to do the same. Taking a bandana from his pocket, he put it under his chin to stem the steady drip of blood.

"You got lucky this time, Caraway, but I'll be seeing you again, count on it."

"Next time, O'Bannion, there'll be no conversation."

The two men walked over to their vehicle and got in. Denny sat in his truck and watched them drive away. After they were out of sight, he took his hand off the forty-four lying on the seat next to him, where he had pulled it from under a cloth. He picked up the piece of cotton to wipe O'Bannion's blood off his hand.

Starting up the truck, Denny slowly pulled out of the parking lot and headed to the highway. He didn't think about the incident again, but the cold, hard feeling the incident had brought forth didn't fade for a while.

Chapter Six

By the time Denny arrived in Salcha, it was as if the encounter with O'Bannion had never happened. Caraway had come to expect potentially life-threatening experiences from years of living in the wilderness. The incident in the parking lot was merely another such episode to him.

He would have gone to see Charlie at the cafe, as he usually did when in Salcha, but it was late, and Denny was anxious to get home. Despite the winter darkness, instead of settling into the trailer for the evening, he loaded up his freighter sled, stashed his gear in the snow machine's rear carrier, changed into his trail clothes, and rode out to the trailhead. The fact that he would have to travel many miles through snow-filled woods at night to get home didn't faze him. He was headed to Lanyard Creek, and that was it.

As soon as he was off the road and well into the bush, Caraway was glad he hadn't waited until morning. There was an almost-full moon, the snow was in great shape to ride on, and the ten-below-zero temperature was fine for traveling too, at least for a man who was accustomed to much colder temperatures. He'd have no trouble staying awake, either.

Denny remembered a particular night, when he was struggling to keep warm in the tiny cabin he had been living in. The old sheet metal stove was working hard, but the little cabin had frost inside, on the wall farthest from the stove. Denny sat on his hard, wood-framed bed, barely big enough for even his spare frame. He was wrapped in a wool blanket, with insulated boots on his feet, and rabbit skin gloves to keep his hands warm, which made holding the cup of tea a little difficult.

The mug had been hot a few minutes before, but even holding it in his gloved hands couldn't keep the tea from rapidly cooling. He didn't have a thermometer, but Denny knew from all the Alaska winters he had lived through, it was at least forty-five below zero and possibly colder. But the rugged homesteader endured and survived.

Caraway knew if a bad moment had overtaken him in those times, if some incident brought him low mentally or physically hurt him, stripped him of his desire or ability to continue, in such extreme conditions it would have only taken minutes for him to succumb. But, his fortitude overcame the reason he was existing the way he was and kept him from giving in completely to grief.

Every winter morning found him doing what he had to do to stay alive, finding food, cutting and splitting more wood for warmth, and melting snow for water to cook and wash his face. Denny carried on.

Now, he was once again on the trail to his homestead. The farther he rode, the better he felt, as if the familiar route was renewing him, clearing away dust and shadows from his mind.

The wee hours of the morning found him pulling into the clearing in front of his log cabin. Shutting down the machine, he sat, despite being cold after the long ride, appreciating his return home.

Stepping off the snow machine, he walked into the cold cabin and lit the kindling pile in the woodstove. Once it was going well, Denny added larger pieces of split birch, before going outside to unload and bring everything into the cabin.

Denny started a fire in the fireplace also. Within an hour, the cabin was warm enough from the two fires for him to remove his parka. But instead, he slipped on his snowshoes and walked up the low ridge to his wife's unmarked grave, under its pure white covering of snow. He stood silently, his head bowed. After a few minutes, he said, "I'm home, Gwen."

Turning away, he walked down the slope again and was at the cabin door when he heard wolves howling in the distance. He stood quietly listening to the calls, so familiar to him he often knew what they meant. Perhaps it was because Caraway lived, despite all his equipment and supplies, as they did, every time he stepped out into the trees.

Returning to the warmth of the cabin and hanging up his parka, he made himself a little meal, drank a cup of Labrador tea, added wood to the stove for the night, then climbed into the large, comfortable bed. This time he stayed there, only his boots and socks on the floor.

Chapter Seven

Denny Caraway spent the rest of the winter doing necessary chores, spending much time hauling and splitting firewood to add to the small reserves stacked behind the cabin. He kept the water hole open in the ice-covered creek and cleared paths through the snow around the homestead.

He hunted small game, ptarmigan and rabbits, to supplement his store of moose meat. Several times he fished through the ice on the lake behind his land for lake trout, grayling, and an occasional Dolly. He loved fish cooked with butter or bacon grease, lemon juice when available, with onion slices and a little pepper.

Caraway was attuned to the seasons as if they were a part of him. He knew the very day spring break-up arrived. One morning, he stepped outside the door to let the chill wake him. Denny knew, from the feel of the air, that winter had slipped away. The deep cold was now behind him, at least for another six months.

Denny was soon able to set aside his heavy winter clothing, but spring break-up called for patience, because traveling was virtually impossible until most of the snow, already turning to mush, was gone.

Caraway spent more time indoors, waiting for clear ground. He had bought a number of used books in Fairbanks. Most of them had to do with Alaska, a subject he still enjoyed reading about, even after so many years actually living in the heart of the land. There was nothing more relaxing to him than reading by lantern light, with a cup of something hot in hand, though he had lost the desire for treats. The cookies and licorice he had once enjoyed, even the cinnamon he had liked in his coffee, were now unnecessary. Caraway didn't question why he had lost the desire for such things. He had denied himself these small pleasures while living his meager existence in exile, and he never partook of them again.

One night during his evening meal, Denny was reading an old book called *Crazy White Man*, about a city dweller, as he himself used to be, who went remote in Canada. He wasn't surprised at how much he could relate to, though their lives were quite different in many small ways. He figured, back in the Fifties when the book was written, it must have been harder to survive, with basic supplies often unavailable in more remote areas such as the place where this fellow had chosen to live. Denny had survived on next to nothing for a long time, and he understood.

While reading a humorous episode, he stabbed a piece of moose meat with his fork and popped it into his mouth. He bit into it, and a sharp, deep pain shot through his head. Denny let out a loud growl. He spit out the piece of meat and waited. Again horrible pain assaulted him. Feeling around gently with his tongue, he discovered one of his back molars had broken in half, down below the gum line. Even touching it with his tongue set off more anguish. Looking at the half-chewed piece of meat on his plate, he saw a small piece of bone, and next to it the broken off piece of tooth. Examining it, he saw the piece looked partially blackened, as with rot, though he had not felt any pain from it before now.

"*Great,*" he thought to himself, "*just great*!"

Caraway knew he couldn't get any help. Spring break-up wasn't complete yet, so travel anywhere, such as Fairbanks to see a dentist, was out. Neither the snow machine nor the wheeler was of any use to him for at least several weeks. He couldn't even consider bearing the misery for that long. It was up to him, once again, to fix things for himself.

Denny knew he didn't have many options. He considered trying to pull the rest of the tooth out, but, since even the touch of his tongue was so painful, he didn't think he could handle grabbing it with a pair of pliers and having at it.

The tough old homesteader had been through a number of life threatening situations, including almost freezing to death after breaking through thin ice into a frigid stream and surviving a winter bear attack. But this tooth was causing him the worst pain he could ever remember, even though he'd had to stitch up three gouges in his left arm the starving old bear had given him.

Searching through several stacks of books on the floor next to the bed, he found what he was looking for, a book of home remedies written over fifty years ago, which he had bought at a thrift store in Fairbanks, figuring there must certainly be something in there that would come in handy.

Sure enough, there were several suggestions for relieving tooth pain. One suggested a few drops of vanilla extract would lessen the hurt. Denny had some he used to make sweet fry bread, but it didn't help. Another stated putting a warm wet tea bag against the tooth would help, but it did no good either, the slight pressure only causing more pain. The tooth was too far gone.

He had to get the rest of the tooth out or risk getting a terrible infection, definitely a thing to avoid.

Slogging through half-frozen mush out to the old shed, he rummaged around and found a pair of needle-nose pliers with their jaws bent at a ninety-degree angle. He had bought them several years ago for a specific mechanical task and only used them once, never thinking they'd ever be needed for such an unexpected purpose.

Back inside the cabin, Denny cleaned off the pliers' jaws, using a small wire bristle brush, until the metal shone. Then he placed the pliers in boiling water for a full five minutes, to sterilize thoroughly.

As he waited, Caraway took several good swigs from the bottle of bourbon he kept for general use. The first gulp stung as it hit the ruined tooth, but the second one seemed to numb the tooth area more than the remedies he had already tried.

Denny placed the sterilized pliers on a piece of clean cotton cloth until they were cooled down. He took the small mirror off the wall and propped it up against several books on his table, then set the lantern next to it turned up high, so he could get a good view of the damaged tooth. It looked rough, but there appeared to be enough left to get a good hold.

Taking a deep breath, he put the pliers in his mouth and tried to grasp the broken tooth. But the renewed torment sent sparks and lights through his head. Yelling, he quickly took the pliers out of his mouth, breathing hard. Taking another big draw from the bourbon bottle, he waited several minutes, grumbling and cursing under his breath.

Denny got angry, snarled, stuck the pliers back in, grabbed the partial tooth and clamped down, roaring around the metal device he was torturing himself with. He wiggled and pulled until finally, the remains of the rotten tooth came out, along with a big glob of thick blood. Denny spat onto the floor, then took the piece of cotton cloth and dried off the gap where the tooth once resided. He closely examined the area in the mirror and was aggravated to see a little sliver of tooth still sticking up from the bloody cavity. Caraway knew it was a piece of the root. Rinsing his mouth out with more bourbon, he stuck the pliers back in his mouth, carefully grabbed the last bit, and pulled it out.

It was an almost painless action, which was a great relief. The deed was done, a dull throbbing ache now replacing the extreme agony he had endured.

Going outside, Denny spat out more blood and grabbed a handful of wet, clean snow to pack into the wound. The coldness helped subdue the remaining distress.

Denny then cut a small strip of dry cotton cloth, folded it into a small, thick pad, which he placed into the gap, closing his jaw gently, to hold it in place until the bleeding stopped.

Sitting at the table again, Caraway let out a heavy breath, picked up his book, and continued reading where he had left off, though he found it less interesting and humorous than before.

Chapter Eight

By the second week of May, break-up was virtually over. The warming air temperatures were a pleasure for Denny Caraway, after the deep winter cold. The last several winters had been rougher on the homesteader than in the past, his joints experiencing more aches and pains as the weather grew steadily colder.

The suffering he had experienced in the winters he had spent in his skinny little cabin hideout had a lingering effect, which showed when winter came again. Denny was no longer a young man, the tell-tale signs of age beginning to show, though on the whole, he was still a rugged and fit outdoorsman.

Denny was glad he had gathered a sizeable supply of firewood to season up for the following winter, so he could concentrate on heading north to begin working for Nathan.

While he normally would have brought in more supplies before spring break-up, knowing he would need them for the summer and through early fall, Denny could dispense with the run this time, until he was on his way home again after the African hunt he and Nathan would embark upon in mid-September.

When he thought of going on safari, Denny got "trail jitters," just as he did before leaving his homestead to ride the trail. It was the old combination of excitement with a small dose of nerves, never knowing what might be waiting out there.

But, if Caraway was a man who feared the unknown, he never would have become a remote homesteader, whose every day held some unexpected adventure. Instead, he anticipated what new experiences lay in store.

In late May, Denny loaded up his wheeler and the little two-wheeled trailer, with all the gear he'd need for working. He had cooked up all his perishable foodstuffs, making an extra big breakfast of eggs, potatoes, and bacon, so there would be none to take to his trailer in Salcha. What he couldn't eat, he left in a little pile out back of the cabin for whoever would get to it first.

Having boarded up the cabin and shed windows, he was all set to go, but Caraway had one last thing to do before leaving. He climbed up the little slope to say good-bye to Gwen. He stood a few minutes, quietly talking to her. Reaching down, he placed a hand on the ground above her. Though Charlie Brady had discovered the grave while he was on the search to find Denny's hideout, he never mentioned it to Caraway.

Denny rode out the trail to Salcha. It was a beautiful day. The sun shone brightly, the air sweet and clear in the prime wilderness. He encountered no problems along the way.

Caraway made a visit to Brady's cafe. He regretted not seeing Charlie after returning from his trip to Fairbanks. Charlie laughed when Denny apologized for not stopping in.

"Denny, since it wasn't so very long ago that I didn't know if I'd ever see you again, no apologies necessary. You want a Homesteader Burger before you head north?"

Caraway asked him what a Homesteader Burger was, and Charlie told him it was the burger he had put together for him the first time Denny had come back to the cafe.

"You remember, with the bacon, egg, and sausage added, along with two slices of Swiss cheese."

When Brady described the burger, Denny had no choice. He'd have one, with fries, of course.

Arriving at his old trailer after eating, he expected to see Drew, but the young man wasn't around this time. Denny left a note explaining where he was going and how long he would be away, knowing Drew would watch over his things while he was gone. He left a ten dollar bill on the kitchen counter, writing in the note that Drew should buy himself a meal at the North Star Cafe. Putting all his gear in the back of the truck's cab and parking the wheeler and trailer in the side yard covered with tarps, he headed north to Fairbanks.

Driving up the highway, Denny kept an eye out for the white caribou bull he had seen once before. It had been an unusual, slightly eerie sight, and he didn't expect to see it again.

This time, pulling up to the Barker home held no worries for Denny. Caroline greeted him at the door with a hug and a kiss on the cheek. Her trim shape was immediately obvious.

"You had your baby, Caroline. I hope it all went okay."

"I managed it well enough, but I was glad when it was over. He's such a beautiful boy, Denny. When he wakes up, you'll see. I named him Maxwell. It's an old family name."

"A special name for a special boy, I'm sure. I'll call him Max; it's a good nickname."

Caroline laughed, "I figured you would, Denny. Daddy's very busy, getting all his ducks in a row for this summer. Plenty to do besides building the lodge. I'm sure he'll tell you everything, so come on in."

Denny thought having a baby had been good for Caroline. There was a new energy to her. She looked fit and was apparently happy.

Nathan was busier than Denny had ever seen him, sitting at the big wooden desk, piled with plans and other papers, but not too busy to greet him and sit down with a cup of coffee to visit. They discussed all the work projects, especially those involving Caraway.

"You've been to Kodiak once before with the crew, I know. Well, it's the first place you'll be heading to this season. More development all the time there. Should be a two-week surveying job, with a six-man crew to get the work done. I believe you've worked with them all except the crew chief, a man named Blaine. He's a good surveyor, one of the best really, though he doesn't have much sense of humor. But, you should get on well with him.

You need to know something, Denny. Apparently there has been a problem bear in the general area around the site where the survey is to be done, so be on your toes, though I don't really need to tell you, eh?"

"No worries, Nathan, I'll keep them safe."

The two men talked for a while, shifting between discussing the work ahead and the safari. There were plenty of details to take care of to prepare for the journey. Nathan told Denny he needed to get a valid passport and all the necessary shots. Caraway mumbled something about not caring much for injections. Nathan told him they were a lot better than getting malaria, yellow fever, or sleeping sickness, but it could wait until the lodge was built.

Nathan brought up what gun to take, and Denny told him the Model 71 Winchester with its .450 Alaskan cartridge should be fine, but Nathan was still a little concerned.

Denny said, "I've studied the cartridge's capabilities, besides shooting a number of moose with it. It has plenty of power for everything except maybe elephant. A few of those have been taken with it, too. Check with your hunter next time you contact him and see what he says."

Nathan nodded, saying he would.

"Now Denny, I know you like your clothes well broken-in, but you have to get new duds to wear on safari. I'll take care of it."

Denny began to grumble, but Nathan put his hand up and told him, "If you put up a fuss, I'll fire you, and that's final!"

The grin Nathan had on his face kept things light, but Caraway knew the decision really was final. So, he reluctantly agreed.

They discussed in detail the construction of Burl Lake Lodge. Barker told Denny work was scheduled to begin the second week of June.

"I've hired some very experienced log builders to do the work. I also have a really excellent finish carpenter to do the interior furnishings. He came highly recommended by a good friend here in Fairbanks, who had him do a lot of work on his home, a remodeled kitchen and the addition of an upstairs room. My friend told me the only problem was the work he did looked better than the original rooms. So, I hired him to do some interior work on this place, too. Well, you'll meet him soon enough.

"I mainly want you to oversee the whole lodge project, be my eyes and ears, so to speak, and take care of the guys as always. You'll know what is needed once you get there.

"I tell you, Denny, it's great to have you back. I have a good, dependable crew, but if I had to pick one person to always count on, no matter the situation, it would be you."

"Even after my disappearance?"

"Listen Denny, I know you did what you had to do. There's no need to hold it over your own head, as far as I'm concerned. The past is the past. Let's concentrate on now."

Caroline came in, carrying her son. One look at him, and Denny was hooked. Maxwell was a sturdy looking child, for an infant. He wasn't a little fatty, but solidly built. He had a serious look to him and brown eyes that seemed, even at his tender age, to consciously take in everything.

When the infant looked at Caraway, he smiled a little. Caroline handed him over to Denny, and Max immediately grabbed a tiny handful of beard. Denny tensed, but didn't do anything to scare the boy, who eventually let go.

Denny laughed a little. Caroline gave him an inquiring look. He said, "It's this big batch of black hair on his head. Cute, but wild. You may have a little ruffikin on your hands."

"A little what?"

Denny smiled, something not lost on Caroline. Caraway'd had a very serious look on his face when she'd met him at the door. Perhaps Max could heal Denny from his long isolation and what it must have done to him, being completely alone and unhappy for so long.

"Ruffikin is what my grandpa used to call me if I got into trouble as a kid."

Caroline smiled, "It's obvious you haven't changed much. Maybe as he gets older, you can make sure Maxwell keeps things down to a dull roar."

Denny stopped looking at the little boy and turned his gaze towards Caroline. There was something in his eyes she couldn't quite make out.

"I'd be happy to, C, if it's possible."

Denny had never called her C before. It was what her close friends and Chad, her fiancé and Maxwell's father, had called her.

Eventually, the close conversation and nearness of people, even such good friends, got to Denny. He excused himself and went to his room. In the morning, there were things to be done.

Denny was up before anyone else. He dressed, went into the kitchen, and made a pot of strong coffee.

Nathan showed up in a few minutes, obviously not quite awake yet. He'd been working on plans far into the night. Denny poured him a cup, and Barker took a long swallow. He gave a little upward jerk of his head. "Good Lord, Caraway, did you put some turpentine in the pot?"

"Well, maybe a little." His lip twitched in a tiny smile. "Didn't know you'd gotten fragile since I last saw you. Besides, I've had the coffee you make in the hanger. It's deadly."

"Which is why I avoid it at all costs, Denny. I must admit this stuff you made tastes better, but I'm certain it'll make your hair curly."

They both smiled, and Nathan began cooking some breakfast. Caroline came in and chased her father away from the stove. He and Denny started putting things together while she cooked. They had a very busy day ahead.

After eating, Denny arranged to meet Barker back at the house in the afternoon. But first, he would go to Nathan's dentist, who had made room in his schedule for Nathan's friend. In the chair, Caraway explained to the dentist what had happened. Denny wanted him to check and make sure everything was all right. The dentist wasn't surprised when Denny told him how he had taken care of the tooth.

"Well, Mr. Caraway, I've treated a number of people who live remote. This sort of thing has happened before. Still, I can appreciate what you must have gone through. I'm glad infection didn't set in. You did a good job of extracting it."

"Doc, if I could have gotten up here instead of doing it myself, I would have. I never want to go through that again."

After taking x-rays and examining the extraction site closely, the dentist gave it a clean bill of health. It was well healed with nothing left behind.

The dentist asked Caraway how long it had been since he'd had a checkup. Denny mumbled, "A few years."

"Then, while I've got you here, why don't we do one."

"Probably a good idea, doc, let's do it."

The dentist did the exam and had his assistant clean Caraway's teeth as well. Amazingly, there appeared to be no other obvious problems.

As Denny was leaving the dentist's office heading back to his truck, he was surprised to see Robert Pete walking towards him. Robert looked much the same as he had several years ago when he, his sister Dorothy, and their grandma, Emma, had visited Gwen and Denny on the homestead, several weeks after Caraway had brought in the body of Robert's father, Henry to Salcha, after he'd found him tangled in a log jam from spring flooding, in the portion of the creek directly front of the homestead.

The two men shook hands and talked a while. Robert smiled, seeing the old hunting knife in its sheath on Denny's belt. It had belonged to Robert's father. Robert had given it to Denny as a thank you for bringing Henry back to them.

Robert mentioned to Denny he was out of work, and Denny knew he should talk to Nathan about it, but before he could say anything, Robert asked him to please come and see his Grandma Emma.

"We only live about three miles from here, and I know she'd love to see you two. By the way, where is your wife?"

Denny told Robert what had happened, and the younger man was clearly sorry to hear the news.

"Mr. Caraway, you need to come visit, please. Grandma is not well. I guess all her years and what was in 'em has finally worn her down."

Denny followed Robert in his old Jeep pick-up truck to where Emma lived. It was a very old log cabin which Robert told him had been built by her father long ago. The family had lived there ever since. But now, it was only Emma, her daughter Bess, and Robert. Bess had been Henry Pete's wife, Robert and Dorothy's mother. Dorothy was recently married and living at Lake Iliamna with her husband.

As they walked in, Emma saw Denny, and her incredibly wrinkled face lit up. Denny could see that life had indeed taken its toll on the sweet old lady. She looked smaller and tired.

When she spoke, her voice was thin. "Oh my gosh, Denny Caraway, you finally come to visit. God bless you and your wife."

As soon as she said it, she saw the look in Denny's eyes. "She's gone, isn't she, gone back to her people?"

Denny nodded and the old Native lady went over to give him a gentle hug, patting him on the back with a steady rhythm, and continued doing so.

As Emma comforted him, Denny could feel something inside him relaxing. He wasn't sure what was happening, but it felt good, so he stood still. After a while, Emma pulled away, looked at him, and asked where he had been for so long. Not sure how she knew he had been gone, he told her, as briefly and clearly as he could.

"Going away from everything left a coldness in your heart, Denny, but it will be okay now. Life will bring you back if you give it a chance. You hungry?"

Denny smiled at the sudden change of subject and said he could eat. So, once again, they ate and visited together. There was a big pot of fish head soup going and though it didn't look appealing, Denny had some, finding it flavorful and delicious. There was also fry bread and boiled moose meat. They fed Denny until he couldn't eat any more.

Sadly, he finally had to leave, but he promised to come visit again after his African safari. They were very curious about the hunt. Robert wanted to know if Denny would bring back any game meat. Caraway wasn't sure if he could, but said he would try. He asked Robert for their phone number, in case Nathan would agree to give him a job.

As he was leaving, Bess, who had hardly spoken a word, came up to him and gently touched his arm. As Denny turned to face her, she reached up, put her hands on both sides of his face, looked deeply into his eyes, and thanked him for bringing her husband home. "I always regretted not being able to come visit you, but I thank you now." Bess handed him a beautifully beaded little caribou hide pouch, the little flap sewn shut.

She said, "It has some things in it to give you strength and protect you. Keep it with you always."

Denny nodded, told Bess he would, and took his leave. He would come back after the safari and tell them all about it.

By the time Caraway got back to the house, Nathan had loaded his gear into the suburban. Denny put his own work gear, rifle, and clothes into the cargo area.

Looking at Caraway's stained and torn pants with ragged cuffs, he said, "One of these days, Denny, you need to buy some new Carhartts. Those you have on need to be put out of their misery."

"These are hardly broken in, plenty of use left in them. Besides, they're comfortable. But, I do need some new boots. These are done for. I stitched the soles back on a while ago, but they're coming off again."

"Well, we'll make a quick stop in town to get you a pair. I've already ordered you some safari clothes from an online outdoor clothing store."

Resigned to Nathan's determination that he have new clothes, he said, "Sure, might as well."

Nathan and Denny met the rest of the crew at the company hanger where the Otter was parked. There were six men, including the survey party chief Nathan had mentioned, Leonard Blaine. Nathan had said he had no sense of humor, and the surveyor looked it, displaying a dour expression.

Blaine and Nathan talked a bit, then Nathan introduced him to Denny. They shook hands, and Blaine said, "I hope you can keep the boys safe, Mr. Caraway, seeing as there is apparently a troublesome bear around our intended work site." There was a tone in his voice Denny didn't care for.

"I know there is," Denny replied firmly. "They'll all be fine."

Nathan spoke up, wanting to head off any bad talk between the two men. He knew Denny well enough to know he wouldn't take much by way of demeaning remarks. Unfortunately, Blaine was a person who was capable of doing just that.

"Well, let's climb in the Otter, gentlemen. Kodiak is waiting."

Nathan's pilot, Stanley, followed in the Beaver, carrying the rest of the gear and supplies, which would have been excessive even for the Otter, with its already full load of passengers and gear. This was a big survey, and lots of equipment was needed. It took over an hour to reach Kodiak. The weather had turned blustery, and it was drizzling rain as they landed.

From the airfield, they drove to the harbor and loaded everything onto a boat to head over to the worksite. The weather hadn't gotten any better, with rain coming down heavier and the wind blowing harder.

The tide was in when they got to their base of operations. The rain had let up some, but the wind hadn't, making it less than pleasant to set up camp. But all these men had lived and worked in Alaska for many years, mostly camped in remote places. They went about their appointed tasks without needing to be told what to do. In short order, they were all settled in. In the morning they'd begin working on the wild, untouched stretch of coast, to be surveyed for a development company that intended to build there.

Nathan had stayed behind. He needed to fly back to Fairbanks, having other projects to deal with, including getting more building supplies to Burl Lake for his fishing lodge. The builders had arrived there several days before to begin doing preliminary work. Barker wanted Denny to oversee the work on the lodge as soon as possible, so hopefully the Kodiak job would go smoothly and be done on time.

After the crew was settled in their white canvas tents, he took a walk around, to get a feel for the place and look for sign. Though he had good rain gear, the wind and chilly temperature were decidedly unpleasant. As he was walking away, Denny heard Leonard Blaine say, "Hang on there, Caraway, I'll go with you."

Denny turned. "Thanks for the offer, but I prefer to go alone, Mr. Blaine."

"Oh, nonsense, I know my way about, so I'm coming. I'm not new to Alaska, you know."

"Not the point, but if you insist, fine."

Denny started walking, and Blaine took a few quick steps to catch up. Denny walked along the beach, Blaine walking slightly behind him. At least the man wasn't too chatty, which suited Caraway. He had already developed a small dislike for the man, so no idle talk was preferable.

About a quarter mile from camp, they came across some very large brown bear tracks criss-crossing the shore. They were headed in the direction of the camp, until about one hundred yards from it, where the prints went up from the beach and into an area of tall grass, and were difficult to see.

Denny knew the tide had been out for less than an hour, so these tracks were fresh. He got a tingle down his back, warning him to be on guard.

"Come on, Blaine, we're going back to camp." He began to walk back the way they'd come. Stopping, he turned to see Blaine bent over, still looking at the paw prints.

"Mr. Blaine, I said let's go."

Blaine looked up at him, saw how serious Denny was, and walked towards him, not happy with Caraway's command.

They got back to camp quickly. Caraway told Blaine to go to his tent, which the head surveyor didn't appreciate, but he walked in its direction.

Denny walked a wide circle around the camp, but didn't see anything until he began heading back towards the encampment. Arriving at the first tent, he saw something out of the corner of his left eye. He snapped his head around, bringing the old Winchester up to his shoulder. He saw Leonard Blaine walking towards him from the edge of the meadow next to the camp. The man was unarmed.

Denny was really angry. "I thought I told you to head over to your tent!"

"I decided to check things out for myself, Caraway. This is my crew, and I wanted to make sure things were all right. Is that a problem for you?"

"You're damn right it is, Blaine. It's my job to keep the men safe, including you. You're making it harder with your attitude. What would you have done if the bear had jumped you from out of the grass? You don't have a weapon. You're the head surveyor, and I wouldn't tell you your business. If you aren't willing to do as I say to keep things secure, we'll contact Nathan, to get it squared away."

"Oh, you think Barker would be willing to give up his head surveyor to make you feel more secure?"

Denny's anger flared at Blaine's attempt to belittle him, but the job was just starting, so he bit his tongue, saying quietly through gritted teeth, "Why don't you call him on the satellite phone and find out?"

Blaine said he would and headed to his tent. Less than ten minutes later, he came back with an irritated look on his face. He stood glaring at Denny, getting the Caraway stare in return. Blaine finally blinked. He said, in a sour voice, that Nathan had told him he needed to do whatever Caraway thought best for safety's sake, and Denny would leave him alone to do his surveying. Without another word, the crew chief walked away to his tent, staying there for the rest of the night.

The next day the rain had stopped, the wind settled down to a steady, light breeze. The crew got busy. Work went well for a week. Nothing was seen of the problem bear, but if there was something Denny wasn't, it was complacent. He kept alert. At the end of the eighth day at the worksite he took one last look around before calling it a day, but as he turned, Caraway thought he saw a slight movement about two hundred yards away near some alders, but he couldn't be sure at that distance if it was something to cause concern.

Caraway didn't care for this situation at all and got little sleep, leaving his tent to patrol the area several times during the night.

Work went well the next day. Without being obvious, Denny continued to oversee everything. He had to admit Blaine knew his business, and the crew worked well under his supervision.

Around three o'clock, while Denny was watching one surveying team, a surveyor from the other group came running up to Denny, looking upset, asking him to come back to where he had been working. The two men trotted over to the site.

When they got there, the two other surveyors were standing still, staring into the high grass ahead of them. The wind had let up. As they hurried to the work site, the man told Denny a very big brownie had bluff charged the man closest to the tall grass. None of the men had weapons, but the guy who had been charged wouldn't have had a chance to fire anyway. Luckily, the bear had turned and walked back into the grass after growling and popping its jaws at the hapless man.

As Caraway listened to the men telling him what they had seen, Denny rubbed the old scars on his left upper arm, from the wounds received during the winter bear encounter years before. Rubbing them if there was a dangerous situation had become a habit with him.

Telling the men to go back to the main camp while he checked out the area, Denny walked slowly into the tall grass. One of the guys tapped another on the arm and pointed to where Caraway had slipped from view.

"We've both worked with Caraway before. He's a really skookum guy. But, he wouldn't have walked into tall grass like that before he left the job a couple of years ago. I heard he'd disappeared into the woods for some reason. It seemed a wacky thing to do. I wonder if he's gotten bushy living out on his remote homestead."

"I don't know man," the surveyor named Tanner said, "but, you remember the big bison that came into camp up at the Farewell Burn job? Caraway kept a safe distance, but he wasn't afraid of the big bull. He knew what to do, and it turned out all right. I'll trust to his instincts."

Caraway stood in the head-high grass, staring at the vague trail where something large had passed through. He remained absolutely still, listening. Caraway knew the big bear was out there and not too far away. He sensed the bear knew he was there, too. They were feeling each other out, despite the intervening screen of vegetation.

Denny got a tiny whiff of scent on the air. It was unmistakable. In a low voice, he said, "Not my crew, bear. Keep your distance."

He slowly turned and walked back to the camp. Caraway told the men it was okay to go back to work, then stood close watch while the men surveyed. With Denny there, the men could focus on their job and not be concerned. Not too much, anyway.

Work continued without another incident. Denny was beginning to think the brownie had decided to just let things be, but being an experienced outdoorsman, he remained cautious.

Three days after the surveyors had been bluff charged, the bear made his move.

The final section of surveying was underway, down on the beach. It was another overcast, blustery day. Denny was standing with his rifle resting in the crook of his arm. He was staring out to sea, thinking about the safari he and Nathan would go on in the fall. He looked forward to it, certain that Africa would provide some interesting moments.

Sensing danger, he turned around, to see a huge brown bear walking towards him on the beach, more than likely the one looking for trouble. The animal wasn't running, but walking with the rolling gait of a big male bear, which shows off its massive power and dominance.

The bear was about seventy-five yards away from Denny and Blaine, who was looking through his transit, facing in the opposite direction. Apparently his stickman didn't see the bear either.

Caraway levered a cartridge into the chamber, stepped forward to be more in line with the bear's apparent direction and waited. He could feel the wind swirling around, so the bear would soon have their scent. His belief was confirmed when the bear stopped, stood on its hind legs, got the wind, and dropped back down on all fours. Instead of turning to move away as most bears would, he began loping in the men's direction.

Denny yelled at the bear, rifle instinctively up to his shoulder. The bear hesitated for a moment, but continued to move forward. Blaine had swung around at the shout, and saw the bear heading straight for him.

At about thirty yards, the bear broke into a run. It would have covered the distance in a few seconds if Denny hadn't fired, driving one of the big bullets into the bear's chest. The animal immediately reacted, turning aside, roaring and biting at the spot where the bullet had entered. Caraway already had another round chambered. Taking quick aim, he fired once more, striking the bear solidly. This time the bear went down, not dead, but fatally wounded. It tried to rise again, but couldn't, collapsing onto the ground, done. Denny stood where he was, ready to fire again if need be, but the giant bear let out a long low moan and died.

For a few seconds, the men stood statue like after what had occurred. It was as if the moment had been indelibly recorded in the history of that tiny bit of wilderness, the men posing in the positions they were in when the bear was killed.

The world returned to normal again. Blaine's assistant came walking up slowly to them. Seeing how close the brownie was to Leonard, he shivered and quietly said, "Whoa."

Caraway, after making sure the bear was dead, had turned to look at Blaine, who had backed up into the expensive laser transit upon seeing the bear coming, knocking it over onto a beach rock. It turned out the transit was ruined, but no one, including Nathan, ever said anything to him about it.

The head surveyor, staring at the enormous dead bear less than twenty feet from where he stood, began shaking. The surveyor was a solid guy, but seeing the bear up close, knowing it intended to do him great harm, had really gotten to him.

Blaine walked over, shook Caraway's hand, and thanked him in a subdued voice.

Denny stated bluntly, "I'm only doing the job I'm paid to do." But then he relented, telling the shook-up man he was welcome.

Denny had made a perfect heart shot on the brownie with the first round. He didn't mention to the surveyor that more often than not even a good heart shot might not stop an aroused big bear immediately. But, the heavy caliber had done the job this time.

Blaine apologized for giving Denny trouble earlier and told him he was glad Caraway was around to take care of things. Caraway nodded slightly, accepting the apology.

Kodiak Fish and Game was notified, and officers came out to take statements about the incident and pick up the hide and skull, which Denny had removed from the bear.

It was noted that the bear had a large wound on its rear flank, a flap of skin hanging down, with raw-looking flesh exposed. It also had two very bad teeth, a common thing with older bears and something likely to make them cranky.

Several days later, the survey was finished, a little ahead of time. Blaine called in for the boat to come get them. The boat arrived and took the men back to the harbor. Several hours later, Nathan and Stanley flew in. Barker thanked the men for a job well done. Denny told him what had occurred on the beach. Nathan suggested to all his men that they take a few days off in Kodiak, saying they could probably use a little break after all the excitement. Nathan would take care of their food and lodging. He was indeed a good man to have as a boss.

Nathan took Denny aside and told him most of the logs and other necessary building supplies had been delivered to Burl Lake. He wanted to fly him there in the Beaver, after spending the night in Fairbanks.

At the Barker house, Denny took a much needed, long, hot shower. Caroline made a delicious salmon dinner, while Denny and Nathan talked and played with Maxwell.

After the meal, Nathan and Denny discussed the lodge, with Caroline sitting in, expressing her enthusiasm for the project. She commented, having flown over the site herself, that the country there looked untouched and was an excellent location.

Nathan said, "I think it's true the forest around the lake hasn't seen many people, so any animals there might be curious. Until the work is done and the lodge is built, you need to keep an eye on things. I'll have to find someone else to be bear guard for the crew on the next surveying project."

Denny immediately thought of Robert Pete and told Nathan about him, vouching for the man. Denny allowed he hadn't worked with Robert before or hunted with him, but he knew the kind of man he was and was sure he could handle the job.

The next day they drove over to see Robert. Fortunately, everyone was there. They were happy to see Denny again and to meet Nathan. Barker got a full dose of the Pete hospitality. By the time they left, after Robert had been offered the position with Barker Surveying, Nathan was in good spirits and very well fed.

Nathan would pick Robert up in three days to fly him over to the new worksite. Both Nathan and Denny had given him a quick course in what he was needed to do.

"So, if the bear decides to make trouble, I ask him to go away, right?" Robert smiled to show he was kidding.

"That about covers it, Robert, besides keeping an eye on the camp in general. Are you up for the work?"

"Well, sure. If I can keep this family going, I shouldn't have any problems."

"He's a good man, Mr. Barker," Emma said. "Robert knows a lot of stuff, and he's a good shot, too."

"I'm sure he'll do well, Emma."

Chapter Nine

As the De Havilland Beaver flew over Burl Lake, Denny Caraway was struck by how beautiful and perfect this piece of Alaska appeared. The winter visit hadn't revealed how wonderful it was. Nathan flew around the lake once, before coming in for a landing.

There were crates and stacks of building supplies, as well as an impressive pile of large, turned logs. Barker had told Denny he'd had the Sitka spruce logs custom turned by a company down in Southeast Alaska, barged up to Anchorage, and trucked to Fairbanks.

Caraway was about to ask Barker how he got them up to Burl Lake, when he heard a helicopter in the distance. As he stood listening, it seemed to be coming closer. When it flew into view, Denny was amazed at the size of the twin-rotor craft and the large bundle of logs suspended beneath it by cables.

"Denny," Nathan yelled, "we'd better step back while they release the logs. That's an old CH-47 Chinook I've leased for the job. I thought I'd have to buy one, but got lucky. The guy flew it up from Washington State, but I'll still come out ahead on the deal. The pilot's a Nam veteran and a real character, like out of a movie, but he knows his flying."

Caraway could see Nathan was right. He knew carrying such an awkward load without any mishaps must be difficult and was impressed as he watched the man finessing the logs down easily to the ground, knowing too how heavy the load must be. Nathan smiled, seeing Denny's fascination with the process.

"You know what, Denny, I think you should go back with the pilot to pick up the last load. Interested?"

Caraway looked at Nathan and grinned. Barker talked to the pilot over his two-way radio, and a few minutes later Denny was heading out to Fairbanks in the Chinook, having been winched up by cable, there being no place for the gigantic aircraft to land.

Nathan was right, the pilot was a hoot. He talked like someone from the Sixties, and wore a tattered old leather pilot's jacket and a red, white, and blue headband. The one time Denny asked him about Viet Nam, the guy went quiet and said simply, "Now there was a far-out event."

In Fairbanks at the log storage yard, the pilot held the big ship in perfect hover mode while the guys below hooked up the cables.

"Since this here is the final load, I told them to put the rest on the lines, man. No need to make an extra run. This baby's had quite a work-out since leaving Seattle. Coming up here was a very cool trip though. I jumped at the chance when Barker called me."

They lifted off very slowly. The pilot didn't seem worried, but said, "Definitely a skosh more than I usually carry, but we'll be fine."

Denny could feel the strain on the helicopter. Though he trusted the guy's feel for his chopper, he was still a little edgy. All the noise and vibration didn't help either. But, soon enough they arrived at the worksite again, and the logs were unloaded. Denny was lowered down, and it was done.

Nathan asked him if he'd enjoyed the run.

"Well, it was interesting enough, and you're right about the pilot being a character; but flying in an aircraft without wings bothers me." Denny grinned, "It just doesn't seem right, somehow."

Nathan made sure Denny had his own tent. After getting him situated there, he introduced Caraway to Roger Benning, the log builder. Benning was a bear of a man, a good four inches taller than Denny and probably running three hundred pounds, but he didn't seem to be carrying much fat on him. His beard was long and bushy, and his Carhartt overalls resembled Denny's old, worn-out comfortable pants, which had been replaced with stiff, new ones.

When Denny and Benning shook hands, giving each other a direct look, they immediately connected as two men who knew the bush and loved being there.

"Denny, it's good to meet you. Nathan mentioned you homestead way down off the Salcha river."

"I do, off a little tributary of the river."

"Really, hmmm. I knew an old fella who lived out there, a guy named George something. I met him while I was doing a moose hunt, years ago. I was living in Big Delta at the time. He had a small, maybe twelve-by-twelve, plywood cabin."

"Small world, Roger. I bought the place from George Levine a while back. It's my ten acres now."

"Really? What do you know. George and I hit it off right away. I was out of the Marines by a couple of years. He and I spent an evening gnawing on moose steaks and BSing about the Corps. He was a hell of a guy."

"Yeah, he was. I still have his photo album in the trailer he had in Salcha. It's a nearly complete record of his life and military service."

"How about you, Denny, did you serve?"

"In a manner of speaking, yeah."

"How so?"

"I turned eighteen in 'Sixty-Eight, but didn't get my pre-induction notice until 'Sixty-Nine. I'd started going to UNR in Reno, taking courses in advertising and public relations. I reported and was inducted. Right after boot, because of my schooling, I was given duty working for the Recruiting Command writing copy and working on posters and brochures for the Army. I served there for two years. My experience in the army is what got me the job I had in Reno, with Wainright & Associates, where I became the head PR guy. I was there until I came up to Alaska in Nineteen ninety."

"Well, Denny, we all played the part we were given. You do what you're told and try to forget it afterwards. But you never forget the guys you served with. At least that's how it was with me."

Nathan had stood silently listening. Now, he offered to show Denny the plans. They walked over to a piece of plywood resting on two sawhorses, where the design lay-outs were held down by several rocks. Roger was very familiar with them and thought they were well planned and perfect for the lake. He was enthusiastic about the project, one of the more interesting ones he ever undertaken. He asked Caraway if he'd ever done any log building. Denny told him about his homestead cabin, describing it in detail.

"Well, if you've built one good cabin, you can build another. Might be able to use your help on this project, maybe building the client cabins. Sound all right, Nathan?"

"If Denny is willing, fine by me. I'll leave it to you fellows. As long as we get it all done by the first week of September."

After Nathan flew back to Fairbanks, Roger introduced Denny to the three men working with him. Two of them seemed fine, but Denny detected a slight smell of alcohol on the third man's breath. When he and Roger had a moment alone, Caraway quietly asked him if this was something he was aware of.

"Hard not to notice, but Craig has always had a small flask in his pocket long as I've known him. It's never been a problem before, but we have an understanding. If his drinking gets heavier, he's through working for me, but no worries at this point."

Denny and Roger went over the plans thoroughly, until Denny had a clear idea of the layout. It became obvious to him this was going to be a wonderful lodge, built to fit into the remote site as unobtrusively as possible. The main lodge was one story, and Nathan had located a perfect area for it, a fairly level site between the shore and the forest, where the tree line was a little farther back from the lake. It would be easy to clear the willows and other low growth there. Craig was to do the grading work. Though he did sip a bit, he appeared to be a steady worker. Denny accepted what Roger had told him and dismissed any worries he had about Craig.

For a few days, while keeping an eye on the surrounding area, Denny wandered around the worksite, watching the men begin their building, noting some of the basic ways these experienced log builders set things up and assembled the logs. They had a system using pulleys and a portable gas-powered winch to move the logs, sliding them into place using split logs for ramps the same as Denny had done when building his own cabin, but the pulleys and winch made it much easier than using the winch on a wheeler as he had.

He was amazed at how quickly but precisely Roger cut the notches for fitting the logs together. He was obviously very experienced. Within three weeks time, the basic shape of the lodge had been laid out, and the main walls were close to completion.

Early one morning, Roger came to Denny's tent with two cups of coffee. "Denny, I've got a problem. Craig's drinking seems to have gotten away from him. He was weaving around some this morning. Don asked him if he was all right, and Craig came unglued on him. Don came to me, and I went to talk with Craig. He was too drunk, in my book, to work safely. I took him over to the cook tent by his neck and the back of his pants and made him sit down to drink a few cups of coffee until he straightened out. I told him either he quit drinking or he would be out. Craig was honest enough to tell me he probably wasn't going to quit, so he's through.

"My question to you is, do you think you can fill in on the building well enough to help us get the work done? I figure if you are willing, you could start on a client cabin with Don, while Billy and I concentrate on getting the main lodge done. After you two have finished the three cabins, you can help finish the main lodge."

"Well, I'm certainly not the experienced builder you fellows are, but I figure Don and I could get it done together, so yeah, I'm up for it."

"That's good, Denny. You'll want to contact Nathan's pilot, and have him come get Craig to fly him back to Fairbanks."

Denny became part of the crew to get Nathan's lodge constructed. He was not happy Craig was a loss, but since such was the case, he was willing to take an active part in the building. Since he had been there, Caraway had seen no sign of any predatory animals coming close to the site, so he wasn't too worried about any aggressive behavior. He kept his forty-four on his hip every day, however, just to be sure.

Craig flew out the next day with no hard feelings. He knew he had messed up and parted ways with Roger on good terms.

Don and Denny worked well together from the get-go. It was obvious Caraway had built before, and the frame cabins for the clients were similar to the ones Denny had built working for O'Bannion several years back, except they would be insulated, with finished wooden walls inside.

It took a little over two weeks for the two men to finish the first two cabins, everything except the interior work, which would include bunks, a small closet, and a wooden counter with drawers beneath it. Don was satisfied with Denny's work and told him he was a natural. He confided to Caraway that he felt it was cheating, using the turned logs for the lodge, but they made things much easier. "Besides," Don said, smiling, "they're still wood."

The weather turned rainy for several days, steady and hard. Roger wouldn't let anyone work in wet conditions, having seen some bad accidents from working on wet, slippery logs. Instead, they hung out in the large tent the builders stayed in, playing cribbage and swapping stories. Denny's grandfather had taught him the game a long time ago, but he was still good at it and ended up beating everyone at one point or another, while they waited for the rain to stop.

Denny was comfortable interacting with these men. They had accepted him as one of the crew. Roger broke out a bottle of Jack Daniels the second evening. Everyone had a drink or two before he put the bottle away. The next afternoon the rain abated, but the bond between Denny and the men on the crew remained.

Denny was actually feeling happy to be where he was with these solid guys, all Alaskans by choice. There had been a number of stories told while they were in the tent, about hunting and exploring in the Alaskan bush. Denny, after his second shot of bourbon, related the story of his winter bear incident, including the way he had sutured the wounds on his upper left arm, saying how lucky he was to have survived. He wasn't looking for a response to his heroics, and the understanding looks and nods from several of the crew were enough for him to feel good about sharing his experience.

Of course, the other guys had stories too, including Billy. He told how he had become hooked on an outgoing halibut longline and pulled into the icy waters of Cook Inlet, descending farther from the surface and daylight every second. He had finally managed to cut the line and make it back up to draw an overdue breath of air. Billy smiled and said he had never gone longlining again.

When the weather cleared, everyone went right back to work. They all felt this lodge project was special. The location, the way the place was laid out, and even Nathan himself, seemed right.

By the time Denny and Don had the third cabin finished and roofed over with green metal roofing, they were able to work together with a minimum of words. After checking with Roger, who was pleased they had finished the cabins so quickly, the two men began building the outbuildings, the smaller one to house the large generator which would supply the lodge with electricity. The other structure doubled as a supply room and sleeping quarters for staff.

A week and a half later, these were completed. Don and Denny had worked hard to get everything finished in a timely way. The long daylight hours of summer allowed them to work as much as they wanted. There was a deadline, and the interiors still had to be done.

The two men were able to join Roger and Billy to get the main lodge finished. It was a complex design, with four rooms besides the main central room, including a large kitchen with a cold storage area for perishable food and the clients' fish. Don was also an experienced electrician and did all the wiring.

Billy had cooking duty and did well at it. They were all meat and potato eaters, but Denny liked salad greens. Being a wise boss, Nathan provided plenty of good food, kept fresh in a large water-proof and bear-proof metal cooler box lying in the cold shallows by the lakeshore, heavily chained to a large old spruce drift log hauled ashore.

Roger came to Denny and told him the men would really like some fresh fish to eat. Nathan had left two rods and reels and a well-stocked tackle box in Denny's tent, so he went fishing, and caught some lake trout and several northern pike as well.

Caraway had not used a wire leader before. The first pike, a large one, had slashed through the monofilament as if it were thread. So, Denny used a braided wire leader next time out, catching an eight- and a twelve-pound pike in a quiet weedy area by the inlet of the main feeder stream on the north side of the lake. He caught some grayling and a nice rainbow about a quarter mile up the same stream, which he named Bent Birch Creek because of a bent-over tree at the mouth. He was going to wander farther up the stream, but saw lots of bear sign, so he headed back, reminded he was responsible for this crew's safety.

Denny walked amongst the new buildings, the lodge, client cabins, and the two outbuildings, all properly constructed by Roger and his crew, including Denny. He couldn't help but admire what had been created. Though the logs had been machine turned, it still took talented, experienced men to build what now stood on the shore of Burl Lake. Caraway was impressed with the way his friend Nathan Barker had designed the main lodge. The building looked as though it had grown out of the forest towards the lake. Its carefully planned dimensions, which Denny hadn't seen in other log structures, gave it a natural, organic look. Even the windows were wider than they were high, and though they were modern and multi-paned, their frames were wooden, and had the look of old-time cabin windows. Nathan was clearly an ingenious and gifted designer, and it was, all in all, a beautiful place. Denny was pleased he had agreed to take part in its creation. The buildings were complete except for the interiors.

But the finish carpenter Nathan had initially hired to do the work had become ill and couldn't do the job. It was the same man who had done part of Nathan's own home interior, and he had been looking forward to having him work on the lodge. Barker was trying to find another qualified woodworker to do all the cabinets, built-in furniture, and trim. Caraway knew his friend wouldn't stop until he had found a skilled man to do the work and was sure the lodge would be finished by summer's end.

Tired, Denny started back to his tent, but he caught a glimpse of something out of the corner of his eye. It looked like a flicker of flame towards the south end of the lake. Watching intently, he saw it again. Yes, it was the flare of an open fire, possibly a campfire. Focusing on the spot and seeing that the flame was consistent, he was sure it was a small, tended fire. Caraway wondered who was out here, in such a remote, hard-to-reach area.

It was well into August, and the dimming light of evening had made it possible to see the fire. Denny decided to go visit whoever was there, early the next morning. Though it was open forest, well beyond the borders of the lodge property, Caraway needed to check it out, an old habit, keeping aware of what went on in his territory.

The next morning, Denny's plan to check out the camp was set aside when he heard the familiar drone of a De Havilland Beaver's engine coming closer.

Within minutes, Nathan Barker's fine old plane came gliding in for a landing and coasted the last short distance to the floating dock in front of the lodge.

Figuring Nathan might have found another carpenter, Denny walked down to the dock to meet them. He was surprised to see his old homesteading neighbor, Andy Larsen, step from the plane. He hadn't seen Andy for quite some time, but he remembered the large, beautifully built house Larsen never seemed to finish constructing, always adding on new rooms and outbuildings. Seeing Andy stirred up a lot of old feelings about those earlier days when Caraway was new to homesteading.

"Hello there, Denny. How are you?"

"I'm fine, Andy, good to see you."

"Likewise. This is something, seeing you again. I didn't know you'd be here until Nathan mentioned you, halfway through the flight. What's it been, seven or eight years?"

"It must be. Let's get your gear unloaded, and we'll talk afterwards. Hello Nathan. Quite a coincidence, eh?"

"It is indeed. Andy came highly recommended."

"Really? I've never known him to be able to run a straight line myself."

"Yeah, and I've never seen Denny drive a nail in true."

Nathan smiled and said, "Well, I can see you gentlemen will have some interesting conversations. Maybe it's good you're in a remote place. I'd like to continue listening to you two haranguing each other, but unfortunately, I've got to fly right back to Fairbanks to get ready for a trip to Hong Kong. A new project in the works. I'll be gone a week to ten days."

Just then, Roger and Don came walking up to see Nathan. He told them Stanley and another pilot would be coming in with the Otter and the Beaver in two days to pick them up with their gear for the flight back to Fairbanks. Nathan walked around with them, impressed and pleased with the work they'd done. Then he walked back to Denny and Andy to say good-bye.

"I leave everything in your hands, Denny. Take care. Andy, I appreciate you helping me out in a tight spot."

Denny and Andy pushed the plane away from the dock. Nathan cranked up the old radial engine and, in a few minutes, was winging his way southwest from Burl Lake.

Denny helped Andy put his tools inside the lodge, then took his personal gear over to the newly built outbuilding, where he would bunk until the job was done.

Denny walked Larsen over to Benning's crew tent and started to introduce him to Roger, but they already knew each other, having worked together several times in the past.

Denny stood by as the two men discussed the building plans. Andy liked most of what Nathan wanted him to build, but he had several suggestions on improving the interior of the lodge and the cabins. Denny said they better contact Nathan by satellite phone before he disappeared into Asia. The call got through, and Andy spoke to Nathan, who approved all the suggestions he made.

Andy was pleased with the building materials Nathan supplied for the work. They were all high grade. Andy mentioned this to Denny, and Denny told him it was Nathan's way, always the best quality.

"Well, I'll give him a top grade job, too. He'll be pleased."

Larsen hadn't said anything about it, but he saw the physical changes in Caraway, not all of which he chalked up to him being older. He suspected Denny had gone through something, but he didn't ask. Nathan hadn't mentioned anything to Andy about Denny as they were flying in. The two men were old school and didn't discuss another man's business, unless he volunteered the information himself.

After lunch, Denny and Andy talked about the old days homesteading outside Hazel, Alaska. Andy told Denny about Walt and Mary, who had bought the first homestead from Caraway and how they spent lots of time out at the cabin in the winter, really loving the place. He mentioned they didn't spend much time there during summer because the trail was "too darn rough without a layer of snow," as Walt had put it. Denny nodded, knowing exactly what Walt meant.

Andy said, "You know, Bucky and Monty never did get the remote B&B done, across the way from your old place. They had a falling out over money, not a big surprise. Bucky tried to get me to work on it for him, but I quoted him a cost I knew he'd never pay, and he left me alone afterwards. The open area they had carved out is already getting overgrown. I used some of the logs they left there for milling. Monty said it wouldn't matter."

Denny was not surprised there had been a problem between Bucky and Monty. As long as Bucky was in the mix, trouble would always follow.

"Denny, have you heard about Bucky, about his wife Laura shooting him?"

"Yeah, I did, Andy. Somebody sent me a clipping from the Hazel paper years ago. Can't say as I was saddened by the news."

"Well, Denny, I may have been partly responsible for it."

"Oh? How do you figure?"

"Well, a few days before she put him down, Laura came over to my place. She had visited a few times, being lonely because Bucky used to leave her on his homestead for a week or two, while he did whatever he did in Hazel. The last time she came over, I saw she was nursing a black eye. I pushed her about it until she admitted he had hit her. She didn't know what to do. I suggested, trying to lighten things up, she could always shoot him and leave him for the bears, but she didn't smile. She stared at me as if I'd given her a serious suggestion. Thinking I might have set something bad in motion, I told her I was only kidding, saying she should leave him, and I'd be happy to take her into town. But, after a few more minutes, she stood up and left. You know the rest."

"I hope you don't feel guilty, Andy."

"Not really, I found it interesting, is all. Did you know, when I was first living out there, I came back to my cabin after being in town, and I couldn't find my chainsaw and milling rig. It was a Husqvarna Model 51, a great saw for milling. Well, I went over to Monty's place to find out if he knew anything, and while I was there, I heard the faint sound of a chainsaw running long and hard. I asked Monty about it. At first he hesitated, but then he told me Bucky was doing some milling to finish an outbuilding he was building. Apparently he had burned out his own saw's motor and had come over to see if Monty would loan him his. But Monty had turned him down.

"Well, I trotted right over, and sure enough, there was Waters milling a big old spruce log with my saw. I waited until he was done with the cut, took the saw away from him, and told him if he ever took anything of mine again without asking, I'd mill him into a stack of two-by-fours and make an outhouse out of him.

"Bucky started flapping his jaws at me. He told me a real homesteader knew helping neighbors was number one. I told him he was full of beans, and left. It was no fun carrying the big saw and milling rig back home. Bucky never borrowed anything again, but it's why I got my dog Luke, to let me know if anybody was around."

"How is your dog, where is he?"

"Oh, he died two years ago," Andy shrugged. "Just got old, I guess."

"He was a good dog."

Andy nodded slowly and said, "Yes, he was."

The two old friends stood quietly together for a moment, looking out over the lake, before Andy went into the lodge to talk to Roger about some details of the construction. Denny had told Andy he'd give him whatever help he needed, but Andy, like Caraway, worked best alone, so Denny would leave him to his own devices, unless he asked for assistance.

Caraway woke early the next morning, but Andy was already up and busy in the lodge. Denny cooked up a good breakfast, bringing Andy a plateful and a mug of coffee. He told Andy about the fire he had seen and his plan to go check it out. Larsen thought it would a good idea, but told him to be careful.

He suddenly asked Denny, "Do you still make the one-pot meal you fed me years ago?" Andy had been out of food and very hungry. "Goop you called it, right? I remember it had baked beans, bacon, macaroni, onions, and moose meat in it."

"There were several other things in there too, Andy. As a matter of fact, I could fix some for supper, only it'll be ground beef. I hope I have enough. As I recall, you ate about five pounds of the stuff last time."

"Well, I'm not half-starved this time around. Still have the knife I sent you?"

"The Randall? Sure do, see?"

Denny had the Randall hunting knife on his belt. He sometimes used Henry Pete's old knife, but it was more a keepsake now, especially after it had brought O'Bannion to a quick stop in that parking lot.

"I'm going across the lake now, Andy. Should be back in a couple of hours at most."

Andy nodded, but he already had his face buried in the plans, studying the details.

"Keep an eye out for any hungry bears."

Larsen waved his hand without looking up.

Denny hopped down into one of the eighteen-foot, wide-beamed aluminum boats Nathan had purchased for the fishing season.

Nathan had told Denny the boats would have smaller, four-stroke engines, but he saw the motor on this boat was a ninety-horsepower model. To Denny, this seemed more powerful than necessary, but he figured Nathan knew what they could handle. Once he got out on the water and cranked it up, he was soon zipping along the calm lake surface, enjoying the speed and the wind in his face. It seemed to take no time at all to reach the area where he had seen the fire.

He shut down the motor and slipped up to the shore, though he wasn't trying to be too quiet, preferring to let whoever was in the trees know he was there.

It didn't take long for Caraway to locate the camp. There was a small camo patterned tent, a short stump, probably for a seat, and a cooking tripod over a fire ring of rocks. A small bed of coals was glowing, and a coffee pot was sitting on a flat rock keeping warm. Denny could smell coffee.

A stack of cleaned cooking gear, a plate, and a cup sat on a split log being used for a work surface. It looked to be a tidy camp, set up by someone who had done it before.

After standing there for several minutes but seeing no one, Denny called out: "Hello the camp, you've got a visitor!"

Denny got no response, though he sensed there was someone nearby, so he said, "I only came to say hello. We're at the lodge building site on the east side of the lake. Come by some time for a cup of coffee if you like."

There was only silence, except for a chickadee chirping in the background, so Denny turned to walk back to the boat. He knew there was definitely someone there, though he hadn't seen anyone.

A voice very close by said, "You could have a cup here, if you'd like."

Denny didn't react for a moment. He stood quietly with his back to whoever had responded to his words. Slowly, he turned, to see a man standing beside a large spruce. Denny took a moment to size him up.

The fellow seemed to be in his mid-thirties, tall and strong looking, in military woodland BDUs. He had a less than trusting look on his face. His eyes showed the same attitude Denny himself would display in an uncertain situation.

"My name is Denny Caraway, and I'm overseeing the construction of a fishing lodge across the way. I came over to say hello, and yes, a cup of coffee would be good."

"And you wanted to see who was bivouacked close by, same as I would have, in your place. I'm Frank Clay."

Denny didn't take the remark as hostile or negative, only as an observation, which is how it was meant. He stuck out his hand, and after a moment Frank let his shoulders down and shook it with a firm grasp, before pouring Denny some coffee.

The two men stood quietly for a few minutes sizing each other up, trying to feel out the other's intent, Denny sipping from the mug. Caraway hadn't missed the fact there was only one cup, and Frank stood by as Caraway drank.

Denny noticed Clay had a Model 1911 Forty-Five Auto on his hip in a military-style holster. He didn't remark on it, though he didn't think of it as a proper gun and round for the woods. Still, it was sometimes better for a man to carry a firearm with which he was familiar and accurate. He figured Clay must have been in the military recently, judging by his demeanor and the holstered Colt he carried, even though he knew the services mostly used nine millimeter pistols.

"Vacationing out here, Mr. Clay?"

"You could say. I'm enjoying the peace and solitude."

"Well, I don't intend to intrude on your privacy, but you are welcome to come visit."

Clay said, "I appreciate the invitation," then stood silent.

Denny knew the conversation was over. He nodded in return and headed back to the boat. He had learned what he needed to know and had no immediate concerns over Frank Clay's being there.

Instead of heading right back to the lodge, he cruised around the lake enjoying the sweet-smelling air and the beautiful, clear day. He felt perfect being where he was. Even the lake water had a special scent to it.

As he ran along the west edge of the lake, he saw a cow moose and her calf, who watched him without bolting, as he slowly cruised by. Further on, Denny thought he saw the back end of a black bear slipping away into the trees. Nathan was right, this place hadn't seen much human activity. He hoped the lodge wouldn't change things, and animals in the area would adjust to its being there.

As Caraway came around the north end of the lake, he slowed the motor. He had seen a barely visible, narrow trail running into the trees. Turning back towards the spot where he had seen it, he slid up onto the shore and stepped out of the boat. There was, indeed, a foot trail leading into the forest. Curiosity always a strong element of Denny's mind, he decided to follow it for a short way and see where it went. He adjusted the forty-four on his hip and started walking.

Caraway was glad bug season was basically over, though there were still enough mosquitoes and no-see-ums around to be slightly irritating. At least using bug dope was no longer really necessary.

Quietly moving about a quarter mile along the trail, he saw it was once well used, but now overgrown. He stopped once, to wait for a spruce hen to move off the trail with her chicks. After walking another fifty yards, he found himself standing before a small, old cabin. It was still mostly intact, though the roof was collapsing, and its one little window had long ago lost its pane of glass. There was a small creek running about thirty feet off to the north side of the structure.

It was a traditional trapper's cabin, with low, log walls and a sod roof, an ample length of the roof used as a porch overhang. The door had fallen off its hinges long ago, leaving the place open to anything coming by. A small rodent skittered across the dirt floor as he entered. Denny was careful not to cause the roof to drop any further.

There was little inside, but he did see an old metal plate, a bent fork, and a broken lantern lying sideways on the floor. An old bit of bear scat revealed how open to the forest the cabin had become.

On a shelf towards the back, he found several old outdoor magazines, one of which he could see was from the late Fifties, a copy of *Outdoor Life*. The cover showed a man taking aim at a whitetail deer with what he recognized as a Savage Model 99, a once popular lever-action rifle.

On the same shelf was a book with ruined binding and rodent tooth marks on the edges. Caraway was surprised and pleased to see it was a book by Russell Annabel, a well known Alaskan hunter and adventurer who wrote some great stories about the territory, a long time ago. This old hardback book was called *The Early Years*, and Denny decided to borrow it to read. He slipped the book into his jacket pocket and stepped outside. He went around to the back of the cabin, then stopped, because he saw something odd looking, half buried in the debris of the forest floor. He slowly bent and picked it up. It was what he thought it might be, a human jawbone with most of the teeth gone. The bone looked old and pitted. It had a little green moss growing on it and had obviously been there a long time. Searching further, he only found one other bone, an arm bone by the look of it.

Denny cast his gaze at the surrounding forest. Though whatever had happened to the man occurred many years ago, instinctively, he scanned the trees.

Denny decided he must have found the former owner of the little cabin. What had happened to him to end his life, Denny couldn't be sure. There were always predators around, and they wouldn't balk at making a meal from some unfortunate human. But, this fellow was probably no cheechako. Caraway decided it might have just been the man's time. Denny knew if your number came up, there was really nothing you could do but go, though there was no reason to go quietly.

Denny went around in front of the cabin and dug a hole by a small birch tree near the front door. He placed the scant remains in the hole. On a whim, he also placed the metal plate, the fork, and one of the old magazines in the hole, as well, and filled it in with care. After all, he was putting to rest someone who was obviously a kindred spirit, one who might have loved Alaska as Denny did. He said a short prayer for the man to rest in peace, slowly walked to the boat and headed back to the lodge. Knowing now the cabin's owner no longer had need for it, Caraway would keep the book.

Denny arrived back at the lodge site and shut off the motor. He could hear a saw whining away. Walking up to the lodge, he could see Andy busy at work, cutting pieces of wood for the interior work he was hired to do. There was a stack of at least two dozen pieces ready to be assembled. Denny noticed Andy had shaped some nice decorative edges with the router table he had brought. He was interested in what Andy was doing, but decided to leave him be. As he started for his tent, Andy yelled out, "What's a man have to do to get some grub around here?"

Denny smiled and said, "Coming right up, Mr. Larsen."

He went over to the food locker and picked out a can of Spam, some bread, mayonnaise, and some half-wilted lettuce. In a few minutes, he had a thick sandwich for each of them. Opening a can of baked beans and sticking two spoons into it, he carried it over to the lodge with the sandwiches.

Denny and Andy sat on the sill of the lodge's double front doors, devouring the sandwiches and beans. They talked about life in general, and Andy filled Denny in on what he was doing. He told Caraway he could actually use some help assembling the cabinets, if he wouldn't mind, to make sure everything got done on time.

Denny said he would be happy to help, and Andy showed him what he needed to have done.

Days moved along smoothly. Denny and Andy worked together getting the main cabinets up in the lodge kitchen. It was fascinating to watch Larsen putting things together. Denny was able to help him with it, but he was still impressed with how quickly things got built. He realized Larsen could probably do this work in his sleep. He had considered Andy an interesting neighbor while living at the old homestead outside Hazel. Now, he could see there was a lot more to the man than he had assumed.

Andy was also a good cribbage player, and Denny was hard put to hold his own, as they played in the evenings after supper.

One morning, Andy asked Denny if they could go fishing. He needed a break from the sawdust and noise. So, they gathered the fishing gear and headed out to the middle of the lake to see if they could catch a couple of lake trout. Trolling slowly, they set their lines to run deep and inside of an hour had two nice fish in the boat.

After they returned, Denny and Andy gathered some beach stones, made a small fire ring and cooked one of the trout with a sliced onion in melted butter, in a cast iron skillet. Denny made some fry bread dough, but instead of baking it in a pan, he cut the ball of dough in half, rolled it into two snakes, wrapped each piece around a sturdy green willow branch, and propped them over the fire.

The two men thoroughly enjoyed the simple but delicious camp meal. Afterwards, Denny took out his old pipe. He'd found it in his homestead, after returning there, and bought some tobacco in Fairbanks. Sitting and smoking a bowl in the cabin had brought back a lot of pleasant memories for Denny, and he had been smoking the pipe once a day ever since.

When Andy saw the pipe, he reached into his shirt pocket, pulled out an old beat-up, round-bowled pipe of his own and asked Denny if he could try some of his tobacco.

"I didn't know you smoked a pipe. How long have you been puffing on it?"

"Oh, for about twenty years. You were just never around me when I was smoking."

Caraway tossed him the leather pouch he carried his leaf in, and the two old homesteaders sat back and puffed away quietly, enjoying the perfect moment, relaxing by a remote lake in the heart of the Alaskan wilderness.

Though it was still light out, they called it a day. Tomorrow would be full of measuring, cutting, and constructing.

Caraway was awakened very early in the morning by the high-pitched whine of Andy's portable table saw cutting a piece of wood to proper dimensions. Andy had beat him to it again. Denny would make a pot of coffee after he answered nature's call.

As Denny stood watering the base of a birch tree, he turned his head and was surprised to see Frank Clay standing at a slight distance, politely waiting for Denny to finish. Clay walked up and said he came to take Denny up on his offer of coffee.

"You're welcome to some," said Denny. "Let me make a fresh pot."

"Since you apparently just got up, Mr. Caraway, why don't you show me where the fixings are, and I'll make some while you get yourself together."

Denny nodded and took Frank over to the kitchen area they used for cooking near the lodge. It was a blue tarp affixed to one eave of the lodge roof, with several cords tied around two birch trees at an angle for rain run-off. He pointed out the coffee and the old fashioned percolator, before going to wash up.

Denny began fixing some breakfast, telling Clay he was welcome to some. Frank didn't hesitate to accept, making Caraway wonder if Frank was getting a little low on food. Andy came over while they were under the fly, and Caraway introduced the two men.

While listening to Denny and Andy discuss the work over breakfast, Frank offered some welcome information: "As a young man still living in Montana, I started working with my uncle Kurt, who was a great carpenter. I did it until I joined the Army. He taught me a lot."

Andy replied, "Well, we could use some help if Denny doesn't mind, and if you'd be interested. Ever do much finishing? The cabinets we've already done need to be hand finished with some oil I like to use."

"I really hadn't expected to do much but camp and explore the area, but, yeah, I wouldn't mind."

Andy turned to look at Denny, who shrugged and said he had no problem with Frank helping. Caraway didn't question what Clay had said about having worked with his uncle. He sensed the man was honest, but there seemed a restless edge, an unsettled feel to him.

"I'll pay you a fair hourly wage plus meals, if that suits you. You could even bring your gear over and stay here."

"The work would be fine, Mr. Caraway, but I'd prefer to stay at my camp, if it's all the same to you."

Denny understood perfectly Frank's desire for solitude. "It's fine, Frank, but if you want to use one of the boats to travel between the lodge and your camp, feel free."

Andy took Clay over to where the cabinets waited to be finished and showed him everything he needed and how he wanted it done. The man got right to work. Walking back over to Denny, Andy quietly asked him what he thought of Frank.

"I'm not really sure why he's way out here, or even how he got here, but I have the feeling he's looking for something to anchor to. I don't know if he'll stick or not. Let's see how it goes."

Andy smiled and said, "You're the boss, Mr. Caraway. Let's give it a try. But, there's an edge about the guy, you know?"

As it turned out, Frank was more than just a helper. The man knew carpentry all right. Andy, out of curiosity, had asked Frank to cut some pieces for a cabinet, while he did some planning for the new fixtures he wanted to build and install. Though he quietly checked on Frank several times, he told Denny at the end of the first day, "This guy is good, Denny. He seems to have the experience he claims, and I can tell he's got good hands. Let's see how it plays out. With him helping, it would probably make getting done on time a sure thing."

Denny nodded in agreement and, during their evening meal while polishing off the other lake trout, he asked Frank if he'd care to stay on long enough to help complete the work needing to be done.

Frank thought a minute and said, "I'd like to, but let's see how things go. I actually have some unfinished business to deal with before deciding."

So, there were now three capable men working to get the Burl Lake Lodge completed. They worked well together, and the work flowed smoothly. Frank wasn't quite the wood worker Andy was, but he could competently do anything Andy asked of him.

About a week after Frank arrived at the lodge, Nathan called in to see how things were going and to tell Denny he would be away for at least several more weeks. Denny told Nathan about Frank and what a big help he had been. All Nathan asked Denny was, "Do you trust him?"

Caraway said, without hesitation, "I do."

"Good enough, Denny."

Before he signed off, Barker told Denny that Caroline would be flying in, to see how things were going.

"She needs a break from her routine at home. My ex will babysit Maxwell. Caroline has always liked getting out into the bush for a while. Probably show up in a few days."

Sure enough, three days later, a Cessna 180 flew over and landed. Denny was surprised to see Caroline step out of the pilot's door.

She smiled up at Denny and said, "It's good to see you. How are things?"

"It's going very well, C, moving right along. How long have you been flying?"

"Oh, I've been flying solo for about two years. But, you weren't around to know."

Caraway, ignoring Caroline's remark, asked, "And how's Max?"

"He's doing great, and you were right, he can be a little ruffikin."

Caraway grinned when he heard that.

"My mom's visiting, and she's watching him while I'm out here. A little me time. Oh, who is this?"

Clay had come up to talk to Denny about the project he and Andy were working on. But when he saw Caroline, he was caught off guard. For her part, Caroline was, also. Frank was a good-looking guy, very fit, and had taken his shirt off.

None of this was lost on Caroline. She walked up to him extending her hand and introduced herself, smiling. Frank got an uncomfortable look on his face, shook Caroline's hand with little enthusiasm, mumbled something, and stood there looking down.

When Denny asked him what he needed, Clay said, "Oh, nothing really. I better get back to helping Andy, though he cut a piece of oak wrong, and he's no fun to be around right now."

He gave Caroline a quick glance and headed back to the lodge, while she watched him walk away until he was out of sight.

Caroline turned and looked at Denny, who was smiling broadly.

"What?" she asked.

"Oh nothing, except it's nice to see you admiring the wildlife out here."

"Forget it, Denny. Dad told me about Frank being out here and you putting him to work. I was curious about him, that's all. Show me around the place, will you?"

Still smiling, Caraway took Caroline over to where Andy was working, still grumbling to himself about the wood he had mis-cut. But he smiled as Denny introduced her. Frank stayed busy with the finishing he was doing.

Andy gave Caroline the tour, describing what the rest of the interior would look like.

Caroline told them, "The big table and chairs Daddy bought in Anchorage for the main room will be here very soon, along with several easy chairs and a matching loveseat. Should be a nice place for the clients to sit and relax, after fishing. Oh, what a nice fireplace. Those builders are good."

"Yeah," Denny replied, "they're a skookum bunch of guys, very talented."

Denny showed her into the other rooms of the lodge, including the kitchen, the office, and another one that would be the manager's living quarters, though she would take up residence there when she was at the lodge with Max. Caroline really liked the interior pieces Andy had made. They fit right in with the log construction and were beautifully done.

Caroline stayed and had lunch with the boys. She sat near Frank, who still seemed uncomfortable. He finally got up and went outside. Caroline gave Denny and Andy a questioning look. Denny shrugged his shoulders by way of a response and continued to munch on his sandwich.

After lunch, Andy came over to talk to Caroline.

"Miss Barker," he said, "it's a good thing you've come. I've added more cupboards and several countered cabinets to the interior plans, with your father's approval, and I need the hardware for them, hinges, drawer rails, handles, and such. If I gave you a detailed list, could you or someone else pick them up and bring them out? I need to keep on working here."

Frank, standing nearby spoke up, saying, "Any chance I could fly in with you to Fairbanks? I have to do some business there. Maybe I could help you find the pieces of hardware Andy needs and bring them back. Would you mind, Denny?"

"Nope, probably be a good idea."

Caroline thought a moment and said she had things to do, but she'd take Frank back with her, they'd purchase the items, and Stanley would fly Frank back with the hardware.

"If you're going with me, Frank, get what you'll need to bring with you, and we'll go."

Frank mumbled a "Yes, ma'am," and took one of the boats to his camp to gather a few things.

Caroline and Denny talked while they waited for Clay to come back, mostly about Maxwell and how he was growing and developing, "On a daily basis," Caroline said. "He's an amazing little boy."

After Caroline and Frank had flown off, Andy worked on one of the cupboards, while Denny continued putting finish on the one already assembled.

Andy remarked to Denny while they worked. "Miss Barker shows interest in Frank, though he seems to shy away."

"Maybe so, Andy."

"Does it sit well with you? I mean, she's a friend of yours, and we don't know Frank very well."

"He seems like a solid guy, and Caroline is a grown woman. I'm not concerned. You ready to put this on the wall?"

It was late the next day when Stanley brought Frank back. They had been able to get everything Andy needed. But Denny suspected something was up. Frank seemed in a somber mood and had a troubled look on his face. He glanced at Denny as he walked by, looked away again and went straight to the lodge with the cabinet hardware.

Denny spoke to Stanley and asked him how the flight had gone. He told Denny it was not a particularly fun trip.

"That young man barely said two words to me. When Caroline dropped him off at the airport, he nearly jumped out of her car, and she took off as soon as he shut the door."

Denny was a little worried and gave Caroline a call on the satellite phone, asking her if everything was okay, and had Frank said or done anything wrong.

"He was quite uncomfortable, Denny and wouldn't stay in the house, but slept in the guest house, which was fine. He had me feeling edgy, but nothing happened. Frank made a phone call to someone while we were at the house. He got pretty loud. I heard him say, 'I don't care what you plan on doing to me, sir. I've had enough; I'm through!' He seemed very upset after the call. I'm glad he's gone. I hope you'll be okay. I have to sign off Denny, Maxwell is in one heck of a mood."

"Thanks for the heads up, Caroline. We'll be fine."

After the call, Caraway decided not to say anything to Frank, since nothing had happened. The man had some issues, but they were his business. He could talk to Denny if he wanted to, but Caraway wasn't going to push it.

Denny walked back to the lodge. Andy was inside, and he had begun laying out the new pieces to install them. Looking up, he told Caraway not to worry, they'd "get it all done in time and done right."

Denny assured him he knew everything would be fine, and they got busy once again.

Frank came in, and the three men worked steadily for the rest of the day, though Frank Clay hardly said anything.

Time slipped by quickly, as it will when people are focused on getting something done. Both Denny and Andy were committed to having everything finished on time, and it looked as if they would make it, with Frank helping.

When they weren't working, each man spent time in his own way. They'd have something to eat together, then relax by themselves. Denny would take a short walk along the lake shore or into the woods, Andy would sit and sketch different project ideas he wanted to do on his homestead, while Frank went off by himself. He always seemed in a serious mood.

Andy always got a little antsy if he was away from the job too long. It reminded Denny of how he had found Andy one spring day, on Larsen's old homestead. Andy had overstayed his time out there, well past spring break-up and couldn't leave on his broken wheeler to get employment up in Anchorage.

Andy usually stayed until spring break-up was imminent, when he'd head up to find carpentry work in the Anchorage area and return to his homestead in winter.

Denny had come to his rescue, feeding him because Andy was almost out of food and giving him a ride to his old van at the trailhead.

A week after Frank had returned from Fairbanks, Denny found the man was gone. After a little sniffing around, he discovered Clay had taken some foodstuffs from their supplies. Further investigation showed he hadn't taken anything else. Denny took one of the boats over to Frank's campsite, and he saw Clay had truly left for good. There was nothing to show he had ever been there, except for a note stuck to a tree with a sliver of wood.

It said, "Mr. Caraway, thanks for all your kindness. Sorry I had to leave like this, but I need to move on. Hope the food I took doesn't make for a hardship. Thanks and God bless. Frank."

When Caraway got back to the lodge, he told Andy what he'd found, showing him the note.

Andy said he figured Frank wasn't there for "the long haul," and went back to work. Denny followed Andy's lead and began working alongside him.

Neither of them gave it more thought. They were both worldly enough to understand that a man, camping out for some unknown reason in a very remote location, who obviously wasn't a nature lover, must have some hidden agenda. Clay had left, and the note told them he wasn't coming back, so they let it go. Neither of them ever saw Frank Clay again.

A week later, Nathan flew out in a Bell Ranger helicopter with another one following. They both had cargo nets hanging down beneath them, containing the furniture Caroline had mentioned.

Nathan was very pleased with the lodge, which was close to completion inside. He told Andy he was very satisfied, and there would be a bonus for him because it was done so beautifully. Barker and Denny talked for a little while, but Nathan had to leave quickly, as there was another project he was negotiating for, down in Southeast Alaska.

He told Denny, "Robert Pete has worked out very well. He really is a solid, knowledgeable fellow, and everybody likes him. So, where's this young man you hired? I'd like to talk to him. Caroline said he's a little odd."

"He left, Nathan, about a week ago. I doubt we'll see him again."

Nathan nodded, accepting what Caraway told him, and smiled wryly.

Nathan stood looking at the lodge site thoughtfully. "I don't know about success, Denny. Right now, I'd rather be sitting in a boat on the lake, fishing. Maybe someday soon."

Nathan and Denny walked over to one of the helicopters, and before he left, Nathan told him, "I should be back in less than a week, and hopefully I'll be able to spend a little time here. By the way, everything is set for Africa. You take care."

A few minutes later, Nathan and the choppers were gone, and everything was quiet again, until the birds came. Caraway had begun tossing scraps out for them behind the lodge. A family of gray jays had laid claim to most of the food he left there. They could be pretty noisy, though not as loud and raucous as blue jays.

Another three days, and the work was completed. As a final touch, Andy used his router to create a sign for the lodge, out of the piece of oak he'd mis-cut. On the surface was inscribed: "WELCOME TO BURL LAKE FISHING LODGE." Denny had already set two peeled birch poles upright, on either side of the dock where it joined the shore. He had searched for and found two the correct diameter, with numerous little burls on their lengths. Caraway notched and spiked a cross pole on the top. The supports being done, they mounted the sign on short chains with eyehooks screwed into the cross pole. The two men stood and looked at it with pride.

Patting Denny on the shoulder, Andy said, "We did good."

Denny nodded in response, and the two old homesteaders walked into the lodge, opened a convenient bottle of Jack, and toasted themselves.

That afternoon, Caraway called Stanley to come get Andy the next morning. Stanley had some open time, so it would work for him.

Denny was sorry to see Andy leave. It had been good for him to have his old friend around again. But, the lodge was done, and Andy had work to do elsewhere. They had a good evening together, talking, laughing, and eating the goop Denny finally made for dinner. He and Andy had been fortunate to come together again as they had. It was impossible to know when or if that might happen again.

Stanley flew in early, and the three men made quick work of loading Andy's gear into the fuselage. Andy and Denny shook hands, and then Denny was all alone on the lake.

For the next three days, until Nathan flew in, Caraway had the freedom to roam through the country around the lodge, having no one to occupy his time. Despite seeing Andy and enjoying the company of Benning's work crew, he felt completely comfortable alone in the wilderness. He was tuned in to the forest and did some exploring, finding a lot of sign, moose and bear, as well as wolf. He came across some scat he couldn't quite identify at first, but walking back from the place he had found it, Caraway came across some wolverine tracks, and then he knew whose dung it was.

The night before Nathan was due, Caraway sat in front of the fireplace, a small fire burning for its soothing effect. His mind wandered, touching on those days he had spent in exile. Denny thought that if he had been better off when he was in total isolation, if living there had been easier, he might not have come in, but things just hadn't gone that way. He considered taking his sleeping bag and spending all night out in the trees, but he needed to be near the sat phone, in case of any calls.

The following day, Denny was standing in the lodge, enjoying the way it had been constructed and finished, when the now familiar sound of the Beaver's engine droned into hearing distance.

Nathan cut the engine and drifted up to the dock. Denny secured the docking line to one of the cleats. He was a little concerned when he saw how tired Barker looked. The man had been working nonstop for weeks, and his busy schedule had worn him down.

Denny smiled at Nathan, took his travel bag from the plane, and the two friends walked up to the lodge, where they sat and had coffee, while Nathan settled down from his flight.

Nathan could spend the night and the next day out at the lodge, before having to go back to Fairbanks. He needed to check with his crew, which was surveying for a tract on the Kenai Peninsula just outside the town of Sterling.

It wasn't as exciting a project as many Nathan had dealt with, but it was just as important to the client.

"Well, until we have to go, let's give you a little R&R, Nathan. Tomorrow morning we'll go fishing. There's a little cabin I discovered, that I'd like to show you. I haven't mention it to anyone, but I think you'll be interested."

But, early morning came and went, and Nathan still lay sleeping. Denny didn't wake him up, knowing he needed the rest. Barker came around a few minutes before noon. He apologized to Denny, but Caraway would have none of it. He poured Nathan a cup of coffee, then rustled up some breakfast. Nathan thoroughly enjoyed eating at the large wooden table he'd bought for the lodge.

Denny gave Nathan a little time then took him over to the other side of the lake, and they hiked in to see the old cabin. Nathan thought it was a "fine old place" despite its neglected condition. Nathan could see, as Caraway did, the history the place contained and dignity in the way the cabin was slowly going back to ground.

When Denny showed him the spot where he buried the bones, he explained to Barker what he had found, and where.

Nathan asked Denny if he had found any identification, and Denny said he hadn't found anything at all.

"Then this is as good a way for the fellow to end as any, out here in this beautiful place he probably loved as much as we do."

On the way back to the lodge, Nathan ran out a trolling line while Denny slowly cruised along the lake. They were nearly back when something big hit the line. Nathan had a real tussle on his hands as the large lake trout struggled to break away, but couldn't. When the fish was up to the boat and Nathan had it in hand, Barker gave Denny a look he fully understood. Caraway nodded and said, "I think he's got plenty of life left."

Nathan carefully removed the lure from the fish's jaw and gently let him go beside the still boat. After a few seconds, the beautiful old fish flicked his powerful tail and was gone.

Nathan looked at Denny and said, "What the heck, we can have grilled cheese and soup for dinner."

"Or goop. I made a big potful the night before Andy flew out, and there's plenty left."

Barker gave Denny an uncertain look and said, "What's goop?"

Chapter Ten

Denny was in the process of waking up, drinking some freshly made coffee in his trailer's tiny kitchen. While he sipped from the mug, Denny thought back on how the summer had gone. Being at Burl Lake and taking part in building the lodge would always be a good memory for him, and it had cleared his mind and heart of any dark thoughts still lingering, from losing Gwen. The beauty of the lake's location, and the positive energy from the lodge going up had renewed him.

There was a knocking on the door. Caraway opened it, to find Drew standing there.

"Hi Mr. Caraway, how did your summer go?"

"Hello, Drew, come on in. It was a very good summer. Have you had breakfast?"

"Nah, but don't let me stop you. I could use a cup of coffee, though."

"Well, I was planning on going over to the North Star to eat. Why don't you come with me, and we can talk over one of Charlie's platefuls."

Drew agreed, so they got into his old Jeep and drove to the diner.

Brady was happy to see Caraway. It had been a while. Denny ordered some ham and eggs, and Drew asked for the same.

Charlie asked Denny how it had gone building the lodge. Denny filled him and Drew in on how the summer had progressed. He described how the place looked, in detail. He also talked about the work crew, his old friend Andy, and about Frank Clay, though he didn't mention him in any judgmental way. He simply stated what had happened. Drew was curious about why Frank had come and gone the way he did, but Brady, being older and more experienced in the curious ways people can act, simply nodded and didn't consider anything beyond what Caraway had told him.

"Charlie," Denny said, "you should come out next summer, after it's up and running. You'd enjoy the lodge and the territory around it, and the fishing is very good."

"I sure appreciate the offer, Denny, but I wouldn't want to put you out."

"Not at all, it's the least I can do for you. I've already suggested to Nathan that you come out, and he's fine with it. Maybe at the end of August."

"Uh, what about me, Mr. Caraway?" Drew chimed in. "Think I could go too?"

"Actually, Drew, I was going to suggest you come out and stay with me a while at the homestead, after I'm back from the African trip. Fall is a good time out there."

"Sounds great to me, Mr. Caraway. I'll look forward to it. Yeah, staying out there would be super."

"Of course," Denny said, giving Charlie a quick glance, "you'd have to split a few cords of wood to earn your keep."

"No problem, I'd be glad to help out."

Denny smiled, grabbed Drew's shoulder and playfully shook him. He said to Charlie, "What do you do with a guy like this?"

"Heck, Denny, I'd let him split wood."

The two old friends laughed, and Drew accepted the good-natured teasing, glad to be hanging out with two men he considered to be true Alaskans, in everything they knew and did.

Shortly after breakfast, Denny packed up and headed down the trail to his homestead. Except for the old Winchester, which stayed with him, he had all his gear for the safari at the Barkers'. He needed to see if his home was all right, before heading to Africa, something Nathan completely understood.

Caraway needn't have been concerned. The homestead was as he had left it. Nothing seemed disturbed, and there was no troublesome animal sign about. He only opened up the cabin enough to spend the night, after looking the place over.

Denny made a visit to Gwen's grave in the evening, to tell her about the summer and how well life was going for him. Before walking back to the cabin for the night, standing alone atop the little ridge, Caraway told her he was still being true and always would be.

Denny slept soundly, but he had a dream about the white caribou. He was riding on the trail in to the cabin, and it was standing sideways in the trail blocking his way. Denny tried to go around it, but the 'bou stepped forward and again blocked his way. Caraway yelled at the animal to move, and it jerked its head far back, making a long moaning sound caribou don't usually make. Denny nodded, turned around in the trail and started back the way he had come. He stopped and turned around again, but the caribou had disappeared.

Denny woke up and sat on the edge of the bed considering the dream. He felt like sleeping a while longer, but got himself going. He dressed, washed his face in the creek, ate a dry breakfast, shut up the cabin again, and headed down the trail towards Salcha and, most likely, some great adventures on the Dark Continent.

About a mile from the cabin, Denny stopped his wheeler, got off and went to look at what he thought was in the soggy ground ahead of him. There, in the mud, were what appeared to be caribou prints. They turned out to be moose tracks, but the shape looked different in the soft, smeared mud. Denny scratched his head, thinking this white caribou business was getting a little strange. He shrugged and continued riding.

After Denny got up to Fairbanks and the Barker residence, he saw Nathan had his own gear and Denny's piled up just inside the front door. Caraway could see he was very excited.

"Glad you made it; your timing is perfect. I tell you Denny, you've got the experience of a lifetime ahead of you. As much as I love Alaska, Africa is truly amazing. Let's have a bite to eat, then drive out to the Beaver. Stanley will fly us down to Anchorage for our flight, which leaves this evening."

Denny already had his passport and had gotten his shots and the certification papers he needed. They would get any other necessary paperwork after they reached South Africa.

The flight to Merrill Field in Anchorage, the ride in a van over to Anchorage International Airport, and their check-in there all went smoothly. As they sat in the waiting area to board their flight, Denny got another case of trail jitters.

He didn't know they were going first class until Nathan tapped him on the shoulder as he was heading to coach. Denny hadn't flown in a very long time and never in first class. He couldn't see spending the extra money, even when he was flush. "Our seats are right here, Denny, come on back. I always fly first class. Figure I've earned it, and I think you have too, so enjoy yourself; it's going to be a long flight."

Nathan wasn't kidding. The flight took a little over forty-four hours. They connected in Seattle, then landed in Dubai, for a long layover. Feeling too restless to sit, Nathan decided to wander around the airport mall. Denny wasn't interested in visiting any of the shops at the airport, exotic though they were. He felt like a fish out of water, so he sat in a plastic airport chair and read one of the books he had brought with him. It was *The Biography of a Grizzly,* by Ernest Thompson Seton. As the title said, it was the story of a silvertip grizzly Seton called Wahb. Denny was impressed with the author's knowledge of a bear's life. It was clear this man from an earlier time knew of what he wrote.

He had also brought several other books: the Richard Proenneke book, *One Man's Wilderness*; and Ernest Hemingway's *The Old Man and the Sea*. He had read Hemingway before and really appreciated his simple but elegant style and the way he wrote about nature. He was obviously a true outdoorsman who loved wild places.

Nathan was working on his laptop for a large part of the journey, taking care of business. A project he had completed in Hong Kong several years before, a building he promoted and designed, had put his reputation in a larger sphere and gained him the project he had completed that summer. But Nathan was still a down-to-earth man who loved the outdoors and Alaska as much as Denny did. Now, the two fellows were embarked on a journey uncommon to most people's lives.

None too soon, they were on the last leg of their journey, and Denny, feeling restless, was relieved when the pilot told them they were on their final descent into Cape Town International Airport.

Denny didn't expect Cape Town to be such a large bustling city. People were going at a fast pace, as would inhabitants in any other large city. But, the town wasn't oppressive to him, as a large American city would be. It was full of exotic sights, sounds, and smells, the atmosphere new and different.

After gathering their luggage, the two weary travelers caught a cab to go to their hotel for the evening, The Taj Cape Town. Nathan was right about going first class. The Taj was a five-star hotel. Denny felt totally out of his element in the swank setting, but Nathan, seeing his discomfort, told Caraway to relax and enjoy himself.

"Let's get settled in our rooms and freshen up. Then we'll go to the bar and have a drink before dinner. They serve excellent meals here. You'll love it."

Denny nodded and tried to relax. After all, this was part of the adventure, despite the posh surroundings.

Denny's room was really fancy. He looked around, sighed, and tipped the bellman, who was patiently waiting. As they had ridden up in the elevator, itself a fancy appliance, the bellman made continuous small talk.

Glancing at the rifle case, he said, "Going on safari, sir?"

"We are and the sooner the better."

"I take it city life doesn't appeal?"

"Correct."

"May I enquire where you are from?"

"I live in Alaska."

"Oh, I see. Now I understand. Are you a fisherman?"

"Not commercially, just for my own use. I live in the bush."

"We call the wild parts here the bush also."

"Interesting."

"You must live an adventurous existence, I presume."

With slight irritation in his voice, Caraway said, "I've had a few. Is this our floor?"

"Uh, yes, sir. Sorry if I was being too forward."

"No, I'm just tired from my flights."

After taking in his room visually, Denny gave the man a generous tip.

"Well, thank you, sir, and good hunting."

Denny was glad to be alone in his room. The bellman was a nice enough guy, but Denny needed some quiet time. He decided to take a long, hot shower, a rare occurrence for him. But after he'd turned the water on, the smell of chlorine repelled him, so he did a light bathing with a washcloth, in the sink.

He rested on the very cushy couch until Nathan knocked. They went down to the Twankey Oyster Bar in the hotel, to relax while they waited for dinner. After ordering dinner, they both requested some good scotch, and Barker ordered them a half-dozen oysters each. Denny tossed one back and loved it. They had an extremely rich flavor and slid down easily. Combined with the thirty-year-old scotch, they served to finally put Denny at ease. Soon, he was talking pleasantly with Nathan, making jokes, and discussing the hunt.

Dinner was served. Denny had decided on gazelle in a special sauce with local vegetables. It was a wonderful meal. The meat was extremely tender and the sauce rich, with a unique flavor he couldn't identify. The vegetables were fresh and tasty.

After dinner, they had one more drink before calling it an evening. As they were headed up to their rooms, Barker nudged Denny's arm and pointed to two men talking at the bar. He said one was a well-known American hunter who had been all over the world in his quest for adventure. He was also a popular writer in gun and hunting magazines. Nathan had met him on a previous safari and wanted to say hello.

He suggested Denny come too, but Caraway needed some sleep, having had enough for one day. He would see Nathan in the morning for breakfast, before going out to the safari camp.

Caraway went up to his room and relaxed on the couch, smoking a pipeful of his favorite tobacco. Weary from the journey, he tapped out the pipe, lay down on top of the bed covers and was sound asleep in a few minutes.

Morning found them winging their way to the hunting camp in a twin-engine plane, landing once to refuel. Denny was interested to note that it was a De Havilland Twin Otter they flew in. Nathan chatted with him about the plane, seemingly enamored of all De Havilland aircraft.

They flew into Zimbabwe, to the Nuanetsi region, known for excellent hunting. Denny could see Barker was absorbed, looking out the aircraft's windows as they flew.

"Look, Denny, a herd of elephants. Aren't they magnificent!"

Nathan was right. Even from that altitude, they looked massive as they walked at a steady, dignified pace. One was obviously bigger than the rest, with large, clearly visible tusks.

They landed at the camp air strip, the dry heat of late morning descending upon them when they stepped out of the plane. Denny was okay with it. Though he had been in Alaska for a long time, he'd lived in the desert areas of Nevada for many years, so the high temperature was bearable for him, at least while he was relatively inactive. Nathan didn't seem to notice the heat.

A large, bald, deeply tanned man wearing an old but clean safari jacket, khaki shorts, and low boots came up.

Shaking Nathan's hand, he said, "Hello Mr. Barker. It's good to see you again. And this must be Mr. Caraway. Welcome to Kubwa Safaris, I'm Jan Vermeulen."

Denny shook Vermeulen's hand. He found it mildly interesting to see the professional hunter wasn't wearing any socks.

Nathan introduced himself and Denny and chatted for a few minutes, until Vermeulen suggested they walk over to the main building. It was a long, low, structure with a large main room and a thatched roof. Denny noticed, on entering, there seemed to be metal roofing under the thatched outer covering.

Inside, were numerous game animal trophies and skins on the walls, and heavy looking, dark wood furniture, a long dining table and a dozen chairs, as well as a gun cabinet with some interesting long guns in it, including several double rifles. Most of them seemed far from new, but were obviously well maintained.

Vermeulen was a personable man, but Denny sensed he would be all business out on the trail. He seemed to have an endless font of knowledge regarding Africa and its animals, and Denny learned he had lived in Africa his whole life.

As they talked, Nathan asked a number of questions about Vermeulen's plans for the hunt.

Vermeulen said, "You told me, Mr. Barker, you haven't had luck in getting a leopard. Well, we know of a big tom, about twenty kilometers from here. He has taken several cattle from a local village, and the head man there has been asking us to take care of it. So, we can remove the problem and get you your spotted cat at the same time. We have been setting bait for a while, in preparation, and the cat is quite comfortable coming to it. We've had the blind set up for some time also, so he should be used to it by now. If you're up to it, we can head out tomorrow afternoon about two o'clock and lay up for him."

Barker was more than ready.

Vermeulen handed them the documents they needed to have while hunting in Zimbabwe. They signed the papers and gave them back to Vermeulen to keep safe.

"Mr. Caraway, you aren't hunting, only accompanying your friend, yes?"

Denny nodded.

"That's fine, but since you will be armed and in the bush with us, I'd like to see how well you shoot. Nathan, you can check your gun's sighting as well."

They went over to the huts they'd be staying in, where the camp staff had taken their gear. Denny got out the Winchester and a box of ammunition. Vermeulen was interested in the old lever action, so Denny filled him in on its history and the cartridge it was chambered for. Vermeulen was a little concerned Denny's ammunition might be reloaded, something he wasn't comfortable with. Denny assured him it was manufactured by a commercial loader and completely reliable.

They walked a short distance to a shooting bench. Vermeulen's assistant set up a target at twenty-five yards, because, as Jan said, if Denny needed to shoot, it would be close up and quick.

Instead of sitting at the bench, Denny stood and put a round into the Winchester's chamber. He paused for a moment eyeing the target, raised the rifle and fired two quick shots. Vermeulen brought back the target and found the bullet holes were only an inch apart, just below center bullseye.

"Well, well, nice shooting Mr. Caraway. Only for fun, how about firing at a little bit longer distance?"

Denny told him to put the target out, only this time it was a six-inch metal plate hanging on a short chain from a wooden support. Denny repeated the process, hitting the plate squarely both times.

"Mr. Caraway, you'll be a positive force to have with us, very good, very good."

Nathan had a double gun in .470 Nitro Express caliber. He had used it on all his safaris and was very accurate with it. It was a Holland and Holland he'd ordered from London, actually going to England, to have it fitted to him. He fired several rounds, and it was spot on. He had also brought his .375 H&H magnum for backup and made sure it was shooting to point of aim, as well.

They had a cold lunch of salad, cheeses, and some thin slices of meat. It turned out to be wildebeest and was delicious. They had a drink afterwards, nicely chilled bottles of Zambezia Beer, a locally brewed lager. Denny wasn't much of a beer drinker, but in the dry heat, the cold beer seemed just right, with a rich flavor.

Their professional hunter had a number of questions about hunting in Alaska. Barker was happy to answer Jan's inquiries. He told Jan that Denny was a true remote homesteader. Vermeulen was interested in the life, and Denny, relaxed from the beer and enjoying being in the company of like-minded men, fell right into the conversation. Vermeulen asked him if he'd ever had a problem with bears.

Nathan said, "Go on, Denny, show Jan your arm."

Denny hesitated, shrugged, then took off his shirt. He turned so Jan could see the scars.

The African smiled and pulled up his own shirt. There were four long, jagged scars across his belly. They looked as if they had been very deep.

"Damned leopard got one good swipe at me, a second before my head man Chirikure put a bullet into him and stopped his clock. If he hadn't hit him right, I wouldn't be telling you. Now, I have some good leather armor to cover me from neck to crotch in case I must go in after a wounded one. The spotted devils are faster than the speed of light, you see."

The rest of the day they spent relaxing out of the direct sun, chatting with Jan, and touring the camp. Denny walked past a small group of native Africans sitting in the shade of a large white pear tree, drinking the same beer Denny was drinking. He stopped, and the men turned to look at him. There was one who seemed to sit a little apart from the others. He and Caraway looked directly at each other for a moment. The man raised his beer bottle by way of greeting, and Denny did the same before moving on.

Dinner was served early. It was another delicious meal, roast leg of warthog, served with yams and greens from the camp's garden. There was also freshly baked bread and locally churned butter.

The conversation continued on in the same vein it had at lunch. The men enjoyed nothing better than discussing their passions: hunting and wild places. The evening ended with cups of a rich coffee, Ethiopian Moka, Jan told them. He had a friend who always brought some when he came through. It was the sweetest, richest coffee Denny had ever drunk. The next day was going to be busy, so they all said goodnight and went to their huts.

As they walked together, Nathan said to Caraway, "So, are you enjoying yourself, Denny?"

"I am, Nathan. I'm really glad I came. We haven't even left camp, and it's already been interesting. Thank you."

"Just wait, Denny, we haven't even begun to go adventuring."

Very early the next morning, they had a hearty breakfast of eggs, game sausage, potatoes, toast, and some more of the rich African coffee. Afterwards, they drove out to the bait tree set up for the leopard. They brought new bait, a wildebeest haunch, and tied it up to tempt the cat in. It had already fed several times in the last few days.

With the meat hanging from a branch, they left to check out an area half a dozen kilometers away where a herd of Cape buffalo had been grazing. There was lots of sign, prints and scat. They would return to the tree later in the day.

Denny was squatted down looking at a particularly large set of hoof prints somewhat separated from the others. Jan asked him what he thought.

"Well, from what I know, it might be an old bull separate from the main herd. Must be big. Those are deep."

"Right you are, Denny, if I might use your given name?" Denny nodded.

"If we get the cat during the next several evenings, we might have a chance to find out how big this bull is."

As they drove back, Denny kept taking in all sorts of sights and smells, making mental notes of them, as he would in his home territory, for future reference. It was instinctive with him. Vermeulen observed Caraway doing so and smiled to himself, knowing what it was about.

By the time they got close to the leopard stand, it was early afternoon, and the air temperature was close to ninety degrees. It was getting to Denny a little, but he could handle it. Caraway noticed Nathan still didn't seem much bothered by it at all. He was glad Barker had gotten him a light cotton jacket, shorts, and low boots for the safari.

Getting close to the leopard tree, they stopped about a half mile away. Vermeulen spoke softly: "From here on, gentlemen, we don't speak. Let's be very careful to make no sound walking, and we'll come up behind the blind and slip in easily, eh? Good, let's go."

Arriving at the blind, Jan opened the back very carefully, and they entered without a sound. He touched Barker's arm and pointed to a little backless seat.

After Nathan sat down, Jan carefully opened a small port in the front of the blind where the muzzle of the double gun would stick out. Putting his mouth right to Nathan's ear, he whispered, "Can you see the branch above the bait?"

Nathan, peering out of the shooting slot, slowly nodded.

"When you see the leopard on the branch above the bait, wait until he pulls the meat up and starts feeding comfortably, then take the shot, yes?"

Barker nodded again, and they were all set.

The three men sat waiting in the blind for hours. Vermeulen's assistants remained at the Land Rover, waiting to hear the shot, but they wouldn't come in until Jan called them on the walkie-talkie.

Just before dusk, when there was still enough light to make a good shot, the leopard materialized, appearing silently as a ghost, upon the branch Barker had been watching. Its silent arrival belied the cat's substance and strength.

It was all Barker could do to stay still, his adrenalin suddenly pumping. Vermeulen seemed to know the cat had appeared, and he tensed up a little. Denny, too, sensed something was out there. Luckily, the breeze was good, blowing towards them. Nathan very slowly got into shooting position, barely changing position at all.

The leopard had pulled the haunch up to the branch, jammed it into place and had begun to eat. Still Nathan waited. As light was beginning to fade, the cat stood up from the crouch it was in, licked its lips, snapped his head around and looked right at the blind, the air currents having turned. Before it could leap away from the minute amount of human scent it had detected, Barker fired.

After the silence they had maintained, the sound of the powerful cartridge going off sounded like artillery, and Denny actually flinched.

The cat was gone, though where, Barker couldn't tell. Jan pounded him on his shoulder, making him wince.

"I do believe you've got your cat, Mr. Barker. A good shot, my friend."

Nathan turned and shook each of his companions' hands, a look of satisfaction on his face. After five minutes, Jan stepped out with his shotgun, wearing the leather armor he had brought, and looked cautiously around. He called for the two men to come out. The cat was lying behind the tree, finished. It was a big old tom leopard, a beautiful cat.

Barker said, "Well, Denny, what do you think of Africa now?"

"It's really a wonderful, exciting place."

"But, it's not Alaska."

"Nope, it's not Alaska."

Jan called his assistants, and they came driving in, cheering the hunter when they saw the cat, patting his back and shaking his hand. They sang in Swahili, a song of celebration for Nathan, telling how the leopard was smart, but the hunter was smarter. Barker finally had his leopard.

Even though Caraway was sincerely happy for him, knowing what this meant to his friend, he wasn't happy the big leopard was dead, not being a trophy hunter, though he didn't judge those who were. However, this cat had been marauding cattle, a valid reason for it to be removed.

They loaded the leopard into the Land Rover and drove back to camp where they continued the festivities. There were a number of men and women from the neighboring village the cattle had been taken from. How they got wind of the leopard being taken so soon as to allow them to be waiting at the camp, Denny didn't know.

The evening meal was an antelope roasted on a spit, yams and carrots baked in the fire pit, and homemade bread which tasted like the sourdough bread Denny enjoyed at home. He asked how it was made. Jan said the bread maker spit into the batter while mixing it, then the batter was allowed to ferment for a long time, until it was dark in color and very smelly. Denny smiled and shrugged.

"Since it tastes like this, however it's made is fine with me."

After the food, there were more bottles of cold beer, a nice ending to the day.

The villagers had gone home after another round of hand-shaking and congratulations to Nathan. Nathan, Denny, and Jan settled down to a quiet palaver around the campfire. The temperatures had dropped, but they were sitting comfortably in light jackets by the fire, discussing the leopard hunt and life in general, enjoying one another's company after an exciting day.

Vermeulen was seriously interested in an Alaskan hunt for a big bear and had many questions to ask. Barker did most of the answering, Denny sitting quietly, listening. But Jan asked Caraway about what he called "your Alaska."

"I have read about remote homesteaders in Alaska and the Yukon, but you are the first I have met. I would like to hear about Alaska from your perspective."

Ordinarily, Caraway wouldn't have wanted to get into a long conversation about anything. But, he liked Vermeulen and could relate to the man and his life in the African bush, so he told Jan about "his Alaska", what he had to do to survive, and how good life was there.

The professional hunter enjoyed hearing about homesteading and hunting from Denny. He suggested Caraway must have a wall full of nice trophy heads.

Nathan cast a questioning look in Caraway's direction.

Denny thought a minute, before stating he wasn't a trophy hunter, hunting only for food or protection, shooting any predatory animals threatening his life or property. He said it in a matter-of-fact way, so Vermeulen saw there was no criticism there.

"Well, it explains why you're not hunting, but it is good to have you here, nonetheless. If you ever decide you would like to hunt with me, I'd be more than pleased to guide you."

Denny told him about the wolverine incident he'd had at his Lanyard Creek cabin and how determined the big weasel had been, which had Jan shaking his head.

"We have plenty of depredation here to deal with, but this sounds like one *bikkelhard* animal."

"Pardon?" Denny asked.

Jan smiled. "A tough animal, hard as stone."

"A very good name for a wolverine. They've been known to run grizzly bears, sometimes twenty times their size, off their kills."

Jan smiled and slowly shook his head. "Sounds like I got the name right."

Nathan and Jan began discussing the Cape buffalo hunt they would start in two days.

Denny stood and stretched. Sitting for hours in the blind had given him a case of creaky joints.

As he stood there, facing away from the fire, something in the atmosphere connected with him. He knew there was life all around, in the darkness of night. It put Denny in a feral mood, as if he were a visiting animal from another land, which, in truth, he was.

A lion let out a deep, guttural moan, powerful enough to penetrate and dominate the night. The beast kept repeating the sound, declaring its presence. Denny was caught up in it. His mind shifted to a more primal level.

Walking slowly out beyond the comfort and safety of the campfire, he stood staring off into the darkness, half hoping the lion would come closer. Denny knew about lions, but, as with bears, he had more appreciation and respect for them than fear. He had been too close to the edge, too many times.

He caught a strong scent, unlike anything he had ever smelled in the past. It was a heavy and, to him, dog-like odor. Denny knew it was lion and that it was close. The solitary, unarmed man heard a heavy breathing nearby.

Caraway saw a quick flash of two shining eyes reflecting the fire behind him. He wasn't afraid, but the excitement had his adrenaline going, knowing the lion had come.

As Denny stood there, a hand was gently laid on his right shoulder. He turned his head slightly and saw it was Chirikure, Vermeulen's head man, the one who had saved Jan from the wounded leopard. Denny had been introduced to him the day they had come to the camp.

Chirikure was a very lean, but strong-looking man, who wore a combination of native and western clothing and personal decoration. He wore no shirt, only a pocketless vest made from antelope hide, with some leather designs woven into it. But, it was his face that had caught Denny's attention. Chirikure had numerous tribal scars on his face, as well as on his chest. There was a fly whisk hanging from his belt that looked as if it might be made from a lion's tail. Caraway assumed it was a symbol of honor. Perhaps he had killed the lion himself. He was a striking figure, aware, and self-assured.

Caraway noticed the Bantu was holding a short-handled, long-bladed spear in his right hand. Chirikure quietly said, "You know, Mr. Caraway, this lion might be merely curious, or he may think you are offering him a challenge, in which case there is no way he will lose his position here. So, perhaps we could slowly back away and leave him to his hunting. Mr. Vermeulen would be quite upset if he knew you were out here. Shall we?"

Chirikure had broken Denny's reverie. The homesteader slowly nodded his head, disappointed he hadn't actually seen the big cat, but perhaps it was best to leave things as they were.

Nathan and Jan were deep in conversation and hadn't noticed Denny had drifted quietly away. When they looked up at his return, he told them he was turning in and that it had been a good day.

Caraway noticed Chirikure had returned to the other native men at their fire, but he looked over and nodded to Denny. He responded in kind, before going to his hut.

Denny awoke to a warm, bright morning. Stretching where he lay in his little hut, he began to get up, then froze. As he moved, a cobra had risen from the floor and spread its hood, not more than three feet from his head. Denny stayed perfectly still, watching the snake making a slight side-to-side motion, half its four-foot body off the floor. Denny began to sweat. He'd never cared for snakes, and this one he definitely could do without. As he began to tire of the awkward position he was in, Caraway saw a face peering in the partially open door. It was another of Jan's men. The native stayed in place for a few seconds, then threw the door open, stepped quickly in, and, as the cobra turned to face him, slashed out with his *panga*, severing the snake's head.

As the body thrashed around on the floor, Denny closed his eyes and dropped back onto the cot, chilled through, even though it was quite warm in the hut.

He looked up to see the young man smiling, holding the snake's body in one hand, its head in the other.

Laughing, he said to Caraway, "Welcome to Africa, sir. Breakfast will be ready in a few minutes."

Denny just nodded, dressed, and joined the others for breakfast, though he only had some coffee, not having much appetite.

They spent the day driving through some classic veldt country, crossing the Nuanetsi River several times. But the river bed was dry, the rains not due for several months. There was plenty of spoor there though, elephant, buffalo, cat pug marks, and many types of antelope tracks.

They saw a number of herds of plains game, including wildebeest, zebra, some impala, and on one occasion, a group of five giraffes, which were fascinating to watch.

By early afternoon, it was back up to ninety degrees again, and now, as both Nathan and Denny were feeling the effects, they headed back to camp for some shade and cold beers.

Denny's interest in the different scents he came across in their travels fascinated Vermeulen. He smiled and said, "I've never had a client before who has shown this much interest in the way things smell here, but none of them live as you do, Mr. Caraway. I myself have been alerted to nearby animals and potentially dangerous situations through what my nose has told me."

A nap in the afternoon sounded good to Denny, and Nathan as well, though Caraway first made sure his hut was clear of pesky reptiles. Jan had assured him snakes being in camp was actually a rare occurrence, with the staff scouring the structures and surrounding areas to make sure it stayed safe, but Denny was taking no chances.

The evening meal was another time of pleasant interactions, but as the men had to get up early for the Cape buffalo hunt, they called it a night soon after.

Denny arose early the next morning, ready for another adventure. Leaving his hut, he saw Nathan was already up and walking towards him with a mug of coffee.

"It feels like a special day, Denny. I think we'll have a memorable hunt."

When Nathan spoke, some strong feeling put a knot in Caraway's gut, as when some troublesome situation presented itself. He didn't say anything, not wanting to spoil what might be a fine hunt for Barker.

After a light breakfast, they all loaded up in an open-bed Land Rover truck and headed out to the area they had inspected after baiting the leopard tree. There was fresh spoor within a half mile of the place where they had seen prints previously.

"Well, gentlemen," Jan said, "from here on we walk. Stay as quiet as possible, and keep talking to a minimum, though I am sure you know the drill, eh? You both have a full water bottle?"

Both Barker and Denny nodded slightly.

"All right, let's be off, to look for a big old *nyati*."

Jan set off at a steady pace, not too fast, but a mile-eating stride. They walked through an area with lots of tall grass interspersed with acacia trees, possessing long, sharp, hooked spines.

Nathan told Denny, in a whisper, "These trees are called wait-a-bit, because if you get tangled up in one, it will take a while to get loose from the thorns. Do your best to avoid them."

Denny also found out why Jan and Nathan wore no socks. There were many cockleburs and small, pointy seed pods to get stuck in socks and create painful little wounds in the ankles. So he paused to remove the pair he wore. Jan and Nathan both smiled knowingly, seeing what Denny was doing.

They had hiked about two miles when Jan held his hand up, and they stopped. He began glassing a buffalo herd scattered amongst the trees ahead of them, and after talking very quietly to Chirikure, he pointed at one particular animal.

His head man nodded and disappeared in the direction of the buffalo they had been discussing.

Jan walked slowly back to where the two Alaskans waited.

"We are close to the herd," he whispered. "There is one very good bull off to the right, with heavy bosses and long, low horns. He is a beauty. What do you say, Nathan, shall we have a go?"

Barker nodded his confirmation.

"Good, we'll wait for Chirikure to come back from taking a closer look."

Chirikure came back several minutes later and said the bull was very good, but he had a bad wound on his left front shoulder, probably from another bull.

Nathan said, "Well, it would be good to take him down, if the wound is bad and causing him pain."

"Very good," Jan responded, "let's go. But be wary. He's probably a cranky old man, spoiling for a fight."

They got closer to the herd, but a turn of the light breeze blowing spooked the herd, and it rumbled off, away from the hunters.

"Okay," said Vermeulen, "we'll take a little break here for twenty minutes, before heading towards them again. Be sure to drink some water."

They had just begun waiting for the herd to calm down, when Chirikure yelled "*Nyati*! *Nyati*!" They all went on the alert, but before anyone could react, the old wounded herd bull came charging through a thin screen of bushes, head down, tail up, looking for a target.

As Jan lifted his rifle to take aim, the bull hit him with a sweep of its right horn, sending him rolling into the brush. But it didn't turn to gore him. Instead it headed right for Nathan, who was trying to place a stopping shot. He fired, but missed in the split second he had to shoot, only grazing its right shoulder. The bull slammed into Barker with its massive bosses, propelling him straight back against a small tree. His double gun went flying, and he was knocked unconscious from the impact.

Denny was right across from Vermeulen as the bull broke cover. He had to jump away to avoid the charging animal. But he recovered and turned to see the bull sweep down with its horn and gore Nathan in the upper leg, then yank his head up so that the man was stuck upon it, hanging like a rag doll.

Denny did what he hoped was the right thing. He yelled as loud as he could, the old Winchester at his shoulder. The Cape buff swung around, the movement causing Barker to slip off the horn.

The bull paused a moment, as if to line up Caraway in its sights. It lowered its head, but before it charged, Denny fired a round. The bullet struck just above the bull's left eye. Its head snapped up at the shot, and the bull collapsed where it stood, letting out a long deep moan before it died.

Denny heard another shot as he fired, and when the bull fell, he saw Vermeulen standing almost directly across from him, his gun shouldered.

The whole incident had taken a matter of seconds, but the damage the huge beast had done was terrible.

Denny put another round into the buff. He knew it was dead, but he wanted to be sure, and he was angry at what it had done to Nathan.

Denny ran the few yards to him and found he was unconscious. There was blood coming from his mouth, and his breathing was shallow and noisy.

Jan said with urgency in his voice, "I'm calling for an airlift to get him to hospital."

Denny responded, saying, "Good, but his breathing is very bad." While he was checking Nathan over, Caraway spoke his thoughts out loud about the attack, to no one in particular, almost as if in passing.

"The buffalo really ruined his chest. He ambushed us. Must have gotten a glimpse of us, or our scent and circled around."

Opening Barker's shirt, the two men could see the upper rib cage was all disrupted.

"I hope the plane can get here fast."

"It will be a helicopter, Denny, and will take about an hour each way. It will be coming from Harare. Cape town is too far away. I'll call right now."

While they waited for the chopper to arrive, they tried to help Nathan as much as they could, but about ten minutes later, his breathing got worse. On a hunch, Denny had Jan help him carefully roll the injured man onto his side. He groaned and coughed up a large amount of blood. A moment later, they laid him on his back again. His breathing seemed easier.

Following the GPS coordinates Jan gave them, the helicopter made it to where the men waited in less time than expected, but to Denny, it seemed a lifetime.

Nathan was immediately given initial medical care. Minutes later, he was being flown to Parirenyatwa hospital in Harare, the Zimbabwean capitol, with Denny by his side. Jan stayed behind to deal with the buffalo and to get his men back to camp.

Caraway had no love of hospitals. He'd had more than his share of sorrow in them, but was glad for one now. No matter what was needed, Denny would stand by his friend.

The surgeons worked on Nathan for several hours and got him stabilized. They put him on a breathing apparatus, then called in for a specialist from Cape Town. Though Parirenyatwa was a good hospital, they lacked an orthopedic surgeon to properly repair Nathan's heavily damaged rib cage.

It took four hours to bring the surgeon from Cape Town. Denny could barely sit still until he arrived. After the doctor examined Nathan's injuries, he explained what would happen.

"Mr. Caraway, we will have to reconstruct Mr. Barker's sternum area. The impact of the buffalo hitting him totally separated it from the ribs, so we will replace the sternum with a special perforated titanium plate, using short bars and screws to reconnect the separated ribs, putting them into proper position. We'll used a muscle transplant, a flap if you will, to cover and protect the area. The grafted area should heal well. The damaged area will require approximately two weeks of healing properly before Mr. Barker can be moved."

Denny said, "I appreciate anything you can do for him doctor. Please let me know how it goes. I'll contact his daughter and let her know."

"Well, unfortunately, the damage to his rib cage isn't the full extent of his injuries, as you surely must know. The wound in his right leg from the horn is quite extensive. The doctors here have repaired it as well as they could, but the tissue damage is very severe. They'll give it some time to see if what they did puts the leg on a course of healing, but if not, he will lose it, mid-thigh.

Also, his right lung was torn up by several broken ribs on that side, and they had to remove a portion of it."

"Doc, I know Mr. Barker well. While he will make the best of whatever is to be, losing a leg would be a real blow to him. If there is anything I can do, anything, please let me know."

"Well, it is obvious you are a good friend to him. You being here to support him will play a big part in Mr. Barker's chances of getting well. They have a room you can use while you are here. I'm going to operate on him right away and will let you know how things go."

The doctor left to prep for the surgery. Denny went out to the nurses' station and asked for a phone to make an international call.

Caroline answered the phone and was surprised to hear Caraway's voice. Knowing her as he did, Denny came straight to the point, telling her exactly what had happened.

Of course, she wanted to come to Harare, but Caraway explained what it would take for her to come. The shots, specific paperwork, and passports would take time. Even the flight, when one was available, took several days. There was also Maxwell to consider, what would be best for him.

"The doctor told me your father would need about two weeks before he can be moved. I don't know about physical therapy. I'll stay in regular contact with you and call every day to let you know what is happening. As soon as Nathan can communicate, you can talk to him yourself. Can you handle waiting?"

"If you think it's best, Denny, I'll have to be all right. You being there with him is a comfort."

After the phone call, Denny went over to the ICU room to check on Nathan. He was still sleeping, so Denny went down to the hospital cafeteria to get some coffee. As soon as he got to the main hall, he saw Jan Vermeulen walking towards him. He had Denny's carry bag.

"How is he?" Jan asked.

Denny told him it was too soon to tell, then asked Jan why he had his arm in a sling.

"The damned Buff nailed me hard as he went by. My shoulder joint is a bit torn up, and my clavicle is cracked, but it will be all right.

"Denny, I'm so sorry this has occurred. We will take care of any costs, medical, transportation, whatever. We have insurance coverage for this."

"Jan, it was something that can happen on a hunt for a dangerous animal. Nathan certainly knew the risks. I think I can speak for him in saying you are not to blame. I'm just glad he's still with us."

"In any case, Denny, I brought your possessions. Your firearms are in the safe at Meikle's Hotel here in Harare. I thought it best to put them there. I am friends with the manager. They will be secure until you want them back. Also, if you need a room while you are here, they'll make sure you have one."

"I'm grateful for all your help, Jan. Again, understand that Nathan and I don't hold you personally responsible. Let's stay in touch."

The two men shook hands, and Vermeulen went off to take care of his disrupted business. With his own injuries, there would be cancellations. Denny went back to the room the hospital provided.

It was almost seven hours later when Denny was approached by the surgeon.

"Mr. Caraway, the surgery went very well. We were able to put things back in good order. Now, only time will tell how Mr. Barker's body deals with the damage done to it. I believe his rib cage will heal well with proper care and therapy later. He is off the breathing apparatus. Actually, now it is his leg we need to watch closely. I wish him all the best."

Nathan woke up the next morning to find Denny in his room. He was still feeling the effects of the sedation, but was coherent enough to talk to his friend.

Barker smiled a little and said, "Don't suppose you have any scotch on you, Denny?"

Barker's voice, normally full and strong, was very weak, barely above a whisper.

Trying to sound positive, Denny spoke: "If I did, I'd have drunk it all already. I'll get the nurse."

The doctor was called in and spent some time with Nathan, examining his repaired injuries and checking the leg for any signs of tissue failure. Everything looked as good as could be expected under the circumstances.

When the doctor left, Nathan asked Denny to come sit. Talking obviously caused him discomfort.

"Denny, listen to me, and please accept what I'm saying. I know you've been through a lot yourself, but you have to be strong now, because I know there is something very wrong. Maybe my body can't handle what has happened to it, but I have a bad feeling. I need to talk to Jonathan Franz, my lawyer. Caroline should set up a conference call so everyone can know what's happening. Could you please call her now?"

Denny said he would and left the room. He called Caroline to tell her as gently as he could what her father had asked. Caroline was silent for a very long minute, before quietly agreeing to arrange things.

The call was set up. That afternoon Mr. Franz talked to Nathan on speaker phone, with Caroline on another line.

As Caroline had suspected, her father wanted to change his will. He amended it to give Denny ownership of the Burl Lake Lodge, with enough financial reserves to keep the business running for several years. The rest of his worldly possessions went to Caroline, as before, except for some generous bonuses for his crews.

Mr. Franz confirmed the changes, before signing off.

Caroline was silent for a moment, then blurted out, "Oh, Daddy! . . ."

"Now, now, daughter, none of that. I am still here and probably will be for a long time to come. I simply want to cover all bases, you see. But, there is something I want to discuss with you and Denny."

Barker gave the doctor a look, and the physician left the room.

"Denny Caraway, in case the worst comes to pass, I need to know you will make sure Caroline and Maxwell are all right. I know it's asking a lot, but. . ."

"Nathan, nothing else needs to be said, consider it done."

Nathan wanted to talk to Caroline alone, so Denny took a walk outside. His heart ached. He didn't want to lose someone else close to him, but it was out of his hands. He said a quiet little prayer for Nathan's health to improve and went back in, struggling to put his mind in a better place. Barker was sleeping when Denny returned. Caraway himself was exhausted. He went to his room, fell onto the bed and lay there thinking, unable to sleep.

For the next few days, Denny split his time between visiting with Barker, getting updates on his condition from the doctor, and talking to Caroline. He knew how difficult it must be for her to stay at home, wondering.

Barker had put all his future projects through Barker Surveying on hold, having his lawyer, Franz, who helped with the business, let everyone, both employees and clients, know what had occurred.

Several mornings later, the doctor caring for Nathan woke Denny, handing him a Styrofoam cup of black coffee.

"Mr. Caraway, I'm sorry, but your friend's leg is not responding to treatment. The tissue is not healing properly; it is dying. His white blood cell count is low, and we've had to give him some whole blood. Also, there is a little spot on his injured lung, which is probably a sign of pneumonia. I'm afraid we'll have to take the leg, if he is to recover."

Denny got a chill down his back. He knew this could be the end of it, but there was apparently nothing else to do.

"Doctor, will you let me tell him?"

"I suppose that would be all right, if you believe it's best."

Caraway nodded and went to see Nathan.

After Caraway told him what the doctor had said, Barker lay silent for a while before he spoke, a tone of resignation in his voice. "Tell the doctor to do what he has to do."

Denny called Caroline to explain the situation. She knew, as he did, this would be a very hard thing for her father to deal with. Caroline started crying. All Denny could do was hold the receiver and listen.

At nine thirty the next morning, the surgeon came out to where Denny was waiting.

"I'm so very sorry, but your friend did not survive the surgery. I fear his body had sustained so much trauma, that it couldn't take the extra stress."

Denny sat there nodding, then he asked to see Nathan. Barker's body was already out of the surgical theatre, in a side room. Denny went in, pulled the sheet back, placed his hand on Barker's shoulder and made a vow to him. "I'll take care of them, Nathan, no matter what."

Chapter Eleven

The steady drone of the jet liner as it rushed through the air headed towards Anchorage, didn't help to keep Denny Caraway's mind off the cargo in the baggage compartment. He had flown with Nathan's body to Cape Town and after days of making flight arrangements, signing numerous documents, and answering unpleasant questions from the Cape Town police, he was finally headed home with Barker's remains.

Denny felt numb, filled with an all too familiar emptiness on the sad journey back to Alaska.

He hadn't eaten much on the flight, but he'd had several drinks of whiskey, which hadn't affected him at all. Denny had hoped it would help him sleep. Home was still a dozen hours away.

Caraway barely got any sleep until the last leg of his journey back to Alaska, not waking until the "Fasten Seatbelt" chime sounded as they were making their final descent into Anchorage.

When Denny arrived in the terminal, he called the air cargo company Caroline had made arrangements with, telling them the cargo to be delivered to the Fairbanks Funeral Home was at the Anchorage airport. They would fly it up to Fairbanks the next day. With contact made, Denny took a shuttle flight north.

Finally back in Fairbanks after what seemed a never-ending journey, Denny saw Caroline as soon as he walked into the terminal. The situation had been very hard on her. She looked tired, worn down from the painful experience. Maxwell wasn't with her.

As soon as she saw Denny, Caroline ran up to him, wrapped her arms around him and sobbed, people standing around them looking on. Denny gave several who were staring at them a stern look. They immediately turned away. He and Caroline needed to get to the house, so they could have some much needed privacy.

Caroline finally collected herself, stepped back and looked at Denny's face. She saw the fatigue and sorrow there. Touching his cheek, she said, "I'm so glad you're all right. It's hard enough to deal with Daddy being gone, but if both of you had been killed . . ."

"Come on, C, let's get out of here."

Neither of them said much as they drove to the Barker house. Somehow, the place seemed smaller, with Nathan gone. Caroline paid the baby sitter, while Denny made a pot of coffee. They were finally alone, away from all the people who had no idea what had occurred in their lives.

Caroline asked Denny for some whiskey in her coffee. He poured some into her cup, hesitated a moment, then poured some in his own as well.

The two close friends sat on the couch, sipping their drinks, talking little. Caroline suddenly sat up and turned to face him straight on.

"Denny?"

"Yes, C?"

"I won't hold you to daddy's request. I know you have your own life to live on the homestead. I don't even know if you really want to continue on with the lodge. Maxwell and I will be fine."

"Caroline, I told your father I would make sure you'd be okay, and I meant it. He was my close friend as you well know, and so are you. Watching out for Max is a given. As for the lodge, I know how much having the place meant to him. I plan on making it happen. The homestead will be fine until I have time to go out again. But for now, there's a lot to do. I'm not going anywhere until everything is taken care of. I consider you and Max family, so there isn't anything I'm not willing to do for you."

Caroline Barker looked into Denny's eyes. She saw in an instant everything she needed to see and knew things were going to be all right. She leaned over to snuggle against him, her head on his chest.

"Is this okay, Denny?"

"Sure, C, it's fine." he said. But inside, his heart felt as if it would burst. He collected himself by silently thinking of all the details needing to be dealt with. Barker had a lot of business going, and it would be a real chore to take care of everything.

"*All in good time*," Denny thought to himself, "*in good time*."

Denny asked, "C, is there anything your father told you I should know about?"

91

Caroline gave him a bittersweet smile. "Denny, the things daddy talked to me about might be of some interest to you, but I'd rather tell you what he said after things settle down, okay?" She sighed and laid her head against him again.

The look she gave Denny made him wonder if there was any special meaning for him in what she had said, but he abided by her wishes, letting it go. He put his arm over Caroline, where she lay against him, and the two sorrowful friends fell asleep on the old couch.

Caraway woke up in the wee hours. Maxwell was crying, in need of something. Denny carefully extricated himself from Caroline, gently laid her on the couch, then quietly went into Max's room. The baby was lying in his crib, crying. When he saw Denny, he stopped and smiled, then frowned, making unhappy baby noises.

The rugged old homesteader smiled at the boy and picked him up. He immediately knew the problem.

"Max, you must have let loose with a bucket of pee to be this wet."

Max smiled and cooed at him, grabbing some beard. This brought a tear to Denny's eye, but he didn't pull away. Taking him over to the changing table, he took the wet diaper off, dried and powdered Max, then put a new diaper on him. Finished, he lifted the baby up over his head, but Max wasn't scared and laughed happily.

Taking him into the kitchen and looking around for what he needed, Caraway made a bottle of formula and warmed it up. Returning to Max's room, Caraway sat, feeding the baby. As he usually did, the child drank it all. A few minutes later, he was sound asleep, but Denny didn't put him in the crib immediately. He talked to him about his grandpa Nathan, what a good man he'd been and how he wanted Max to be well and have a good life. Denny stopped talking, unable to go on. He felt a light hand on his shoulder.

He sat a while longer, Caroline standing behind him, no words passing between them, silently sharing their mutual loss. Standing, he handed Max to Caroline, leaving the room to have a cup of coffee. He wasn't tired, despite the early hour.

Caroline came into the kitchen. She leaned against Denny, putting her arms around him. Looking into his eyes, she said, "Denny, I don't want to be alone right now. There's no one else I want to be with, but I don't want to do anything to ruin our friendship. You're the best man I know, or I wouldn't be here, right now."

Denny knew exactly what Caroline wanted and why, because he felt the same. He knew there was more than friendship between them, ever since the time years before, while they were waiting for the rescue helicopter to take them from the site of a bush plane crash she had been in. By the grace of God, Denny had been in the area, saw the plane go down, and was able to help Caroline. The pilot hadn't survived.

"C, you know I care about you, but this wouldn't be good. We have to concentrate on everything needing to be done. I think being together that way would complicate things. I can't say what the future might hold, but right now, we'd best let things stay as they are. Can you handle just knowing I'm here for you?"

Caroline smiled and told Denny she should have known he'd be strong enough to keep things right. She kissed him on the cheek and said good-night.

Caroline had accepted Denny's decision to remain as friends. Still, she didn't completely discard the idea they might share more someday. Denny being years her elder didn't matter. He was a special, unique man, and she would bide her time. Having him as a good friend would do, for now. Nathan had once told Denny, if Caroline got something set in her mind, it wasn't going away. He knew his daughter well.

Denny sighed and called it a night, too. Tomorrow was going to be full of unpleasant but necessary things to do, and he felt drained from all that had happened. Nathan would be delivered to the Fairbanks Funeral Home the next afternoon. He and Caroline would go there, so she could see her father, and all the funeral arrangements could be made.

Nathan's memorial service went as well as could be expected. Caroline had notified everyone who needed or would want to know, and the people who attended overflowed the church. The cemetery was packed with family, good friends, business associates, and the men who had worked for and respected him. Denny was humbled by the love and respect Nathan commanded.

The biggest surprise was Jan Vermeulen driving up at the cemetery. Denny had let Jan know in a phone call what was going on. He also wanted to know how Vermeulen was doing. Caraway was surprised when Jan told him he was retiring from hunting. He loved being a professional hunter in Africa, but, as he told Caraway, "I believe the buff and what happened to Nathan was a sign, telling me it was time to follow another trail. I'm going to be doing only photographic safaris now, a glorified tour guide, I suppose you could say, but it will take care of things for me."

Denny and Vermeulen talked about what the future might hold for both of them. Jan told Denny he hoped they would stay in touch and perhaps hunt together in Alaska some time.

But, Caraway was amazed when Jan pulled up in a taxi and stepped out, carrying a curious item. It turned out to be a small African turtle shell rattle.

He walked up to where Caroline and Denny were standing and shook his hand. Caraway introduced the two of them, and Caroline took Vermeulen's hand, holding on to it. She told him it was very kind for him to come all the way to Alaska to attend the ceremony. Jan told her he was glad he could be there. "He was a good man. I am deeply sorry things went as they did. My head man, Chirikure, has had this rattle in his family for many years, and he asked me to bring it for Mr. Barker to have with him."

Caroline thanked Jan again, before returning to stand at the grave side.

Vermeulen turned to Denny, "So, are you well, Mr. Caraway?"

"I'm okay, Jan. There's been a lot to do, but Lord willing, things will play out as they should. It really was very good of you to come. Do you have any time to visit?"

"No, I have some business to attend to in New York. From there I must head home. There are client arrangements to make, to help fulfill their desires for adventure. In a year or two, however, I would like to come here to hunt for moose and bear."

"Let me know if you schedule a hunt, so we can get together."

They shook hands again, then walked over to the gathering around the grave.

Barker's lawyer, Mr. Franz, gave a touching eulogy at the church service, having known Nathan for many years. A number of others spoke as well. After the ceremony, Franz came over to Denny and Caroline at the church door, where they were saying good-bye to people. He arranged to see them both, for the formal reading of the will the following Monday.

The several weeks that followed were a seemingly endless time of making arrangements, signing papers and giving notices, but eventually all the major knotholes had been gone through.

Mr. Franz and Caroline discussed the best way to close down her dad's business. He already had some alternative plans for solid investments once the business was liquidated, some of which he had arranged with Nathan Barker a few years back. Caroline's father had liked to be prepared for any eventuality. Besides being a very shrewd businessman and competent lawyer, Franz was a family friend, so he would make sure Caroline would get all she could from any sales.

In truth, selling off Nathan's business went more easily than expected. A man from Juneau was seriously interested in buying out all the company's assets and equipment, and hiring the crews Nathan had used, if they were willing. It had taken very little negotiating to finalize a deal.

Denny and Caroline could see an end to all the complications they'd had to deal with, following Nathan's death, and anticipated life becoming more peaceful and normal again.

Chapter Twelve

Denny had just come out of a Fairbanks supermarket with his purchases. He'd picked up some crab legs and corn on the cob he and Caroline would have for dinner. He was going out to the Lanyard Creek homestead in the morning. It had been far too long since he'd been there. Fall was definitely rolling into early winter, the temperatures dropping every day. He longed for his remote home, looking forward to the wheeler journey along the primitive trail to his cabin.

As he carried the plastic bags of food to the truck, Denny stopped short, amazed to see what had happened in the short time he'd been in the store.

The two tires on the truck's left side were flat. There was also a long, ragged scrape along the door and onto the side of the bed. Taking a closer look, he saw one of the headlights was broken out, too. The flat tires had obviously been punctured with a knife, which probably was used to scrape the paint, too.

Denny was righteously angry, as he stood there surveying the damage. Why would anyone pick on his truck in this way? Looking around, he didn't see any other vandalized vehicles. He wondered if O'Bannion was involved.

He knew there was a tire store about a mile away, but it would ruin the rims to drive his rig there. So, he would replace one of the bad tires with the spare, remove the other flat, leave the truck up on the jack, and get a taxi to take him, with the tires, to the store for replacements.

As he began to remove the first tire, a young man in his twenties caught his attention. Denny asked the fellow what he wanted.

"Well, I saw the man who roughed up your truck, as he was leaving."

"What exactly did you see?"

"As I was coming out of the store, there was a Suburban stopped in the lane right in front of your pick-up. A man had just broken out your headlight. He got into his vehicle and drove off, going past the store front pretty fast, but I got a good look at him."

"And?"

"Oh, he seemed to be sitting tall in his truck, smiling, but the main thing I remember is he had a big red beard."

"*O'Bannion*," Denny thought to himself.

"Was his truck faded blue with gray stripes down the sides?"

"Yeah, it was a blue Suburban. Do you know him?"

"Yes I do. Thanks, I appreciate the heads up."

He nodded, started to walk away, but stopped to ask Denny if he could use some help. Denny asked the fellow if he could take him to the tire shop, and the young man said he'd be glad to give him a lift.

Denny's anger had changed. He had gone very still inside. He didn't think about what he wanted to do. If the time came, he'd deal with it without hesitation. The guy who was giving him a ride sensed Denny's dark mood and refrained from making conversation. He was glad Caraway was mad at somebody else.

When they got to the store, the helpful young man waited until Caraway unloaded the tires, then waved and drove off. Denny rolled the tires into the shop and waited while they were replaced. One of the shop workers gave him a ride back to his truck with the new ones.

With the new tires on his pick-up, Denny went to a car parts store, buying a replacement headlight there. The scratched paint would remain as it was, an unpleasant reminder of O'Bannion's foulness.

Caraway drove downtown to O'Bannion's guide service office, but when he got there, he saw the place had become an herb shop. He realized the man must have lost his business after being busted for illegal guiding practices.

The homesteader decided to let it go for the time being. He had a lot on his mind, but there would be, without a doubt, another time and a reckoning.

Driving over to the Barker house, his home for months now, Denny decided not to say anything to Caroline. She'd already had enough stress.

The two had established a comfortable evening routine. After putting Max to bed, they'd play some cards and discuss whatever was next to be done. But now, all the important needs had been dealt with. Life had regained some normalcy.

Caroline had a number of lady friends who visited regularly, giving Caroline a buffer against thinking too much about her father's death and all the concerns that followed. Denny tended to avoid the house if Caroline had company, spending time exploring the area around Fairbanks.

For the past several weeks, he had been telling Caroline, in one way or another, of his need to get out to the homestead. She eventually told him things were on an even keel for her again, so he should go, and stay as long as he needed. But she made sure he knew he could come back any time.

"Like you've said, Denny, you're family."

It was clear the two would miss one another. They had grown even closer since the tragedy.

Two weeks earlier, Denny had flown over the new lodge at Burl Lake with Nathan's former pilot, Stanley, who had begun a charter business for himself, made possible by the bonus money Barker had left him. Stanley was an excellent pilot, careful and capable. After the flight, he told Denny he'd be happy to work for him, transporting clients between Fairbanks and the lodge. Caraway had jumped at the chance to have Stanley flying for him.

Caroline sold Stanley the De Havilland Otter for his business, but kept the Beaver for herself, not just because she thought it a great aircraft for use in Alaska, but as a way of staying connected to her father. He had instructed her on the flying and maintenance of the old craft.

The flight over the newly built lodge had shown everything to be in great shape. It would be ready for business when summer came. Denny had turned the boats over for the winter, with the motors in storage out of the weather, away from any destructive animals. There was already a foot deep covering of snow over everything. Denny had asked Stanley if he would make a flight over the lodge every two or three weeks while he was on his homestead, or after any big snow storm, to make sure the place was all right, though the buildings were sturdily built by Roger Benning and his crew. The lodge could handle a truly heavy snow load.

Checking on the lodge was only for Denny's peace of mind. Already the burden of ownership was beginning to tell on him. Denny knew it was the best way for him to make a living, but it was also his great appreciation for Nathan's generosity that made running the lodge a matter of real importance for him. As the De Havilland Beaver acted as a connection between Caroline and her father, for Denny, the lodge was a living monument to Nathan Barker's memory.

Denny got a case of trail jitters at the thought of having a business of his own to open for the first time. It had been wonderful to see the lodge going up the past summer, though he never dreamed he would actually own it.

He reminded himself he'd need to talk to Charlie Brady for advice on what food to order for feeding the clients, since there was already a growing list of people who wanted to come fish the lake and enjoy the beauty of the surrounding wilderness.

Caroline was handling the reservations, and booking for the coming season was nearly complete. She knew what her father required of anyone coming out to the lodge, as far as their outdoor and fishing experience was concerned.

She was terrific dealing with people and had even booked a man from France, Marcel Durier, who had fished all over the world. He'd met and become friends with Nathan during his very first safari to Africa, where Marcel was fishing for exotic African fish species. Nathan had written down Marcel's contact information. Caroline had called to offer him one of the very first fishing reservations, saying, though her father was no longer with them, she knew he'd be pleased to have him there. Hearing of Barker's demise, Durier said he would be honored to fish at the lodge.

Denny knew having Caroline and Max out at the lodge during the season would be good for them, as well as for the lodge's business. In her own way, she loved Alaska as much as Denny did, and he knew she was looking forward to the first season, too.

One of the men who had worked for years on Barker's survey crews, Everett Tanner, had come by the Fairbanks house to offer his condolences. Caroline had met him before, on several occasions and knew her father liked the man. Knowing he probably needed work in the off season, she offered him winter employment, keeping the place cleared of snow and generally maintained. He agreed without hesitation, appreciating the offer. Tanner would go back to surveying again in the spring for the man who had bought Nathan's surveying business, but until then, he would have had to hang on through the winter, a typical situation in Alaska. There was a small guest cabin behind the big log home, so he'd have a place to stay in addition to a decent salary.

Denny took the man aside during the visit, asking to be told if anything wasn't going right for Caroline, so he could come deal with it. The man assured him he would. Caraway gave Charlie Brady's number at the North Star Cafe to Tanner, telling him Charlie could contact him over the VHF radio he had bought to install at the Lanyard Creek homestead.

Another purchase Denny had made since living in Fairbanks was a small, easy to install solar power system for his homestead. It consisted of two panels, an inverter, a small control panel, and two large deep-cycle batteries. This way he could keep the VHF radio running in case of emergencies. He also bought two twelve-volt boat cabin lights so he could have light in the dark months of winter, without having to use the kerosene lanterns. In addition, he bought a reliable generator for back-up charging of the batteries. When he went back to the homestead, he'd haul in everything with him.

Denny did not consider "modernizing" his homestead a sign he couldn't handle the daily tasks of homesteading any more. He simply saw no valid reason, especially at his age, to make life harder than necessary. Caraway had nothing to prove to anyone, especially himself. He saw improving the place as a means of making life easier on the 'stead.

After winter was truly in, Denny couldn't put off going out to his homestead any longer. It was difficult to leave Caroline and Max, even though he knew they would be fine. Caroline was a strong, capable person, but Caraway was a man of his word. The vow he made to Nathan was as strong in his mind as it had been the day he had made it, months ago, in the distant land that had initially brought excitement and adventure to the two men, but ultimately, great sorrow.

Caroline, as an affectionate gesture, had packed Denny a meal in a brown paper bag for the ride in to his homestead. He smiled, gave her arm a little squeeze, playfully tugged on Max's ear and left.

Chapter Thirteen

As Denny rode the trail to his cabin, the burden he had labored under since that fateful journey to Africa faded away. His senses became keener, as they did whenever he left civilized ground. He was back in his home territory, even though the homestead was still many miles away.

The snow machine he was using was one of several kept at the Fairbanks house. Denny, having come out the trail on his wheeler in late spring, needed a snow machine to get back in now. Caroline had simply told him to load one of the Skidoos into the back of his truck and "not worry about it."

After traveling for a while, Denny found it interesting there were no hoof or paw prints, snow machine tracks or otherwise disturbed snow to show anyone else, two-legged or four, had been on the trail. He smiled to himself, considering this a sign that there was nothing unpleasant or negative waiting for him.

It was dark by the time he reached his home. As he'd expected, the trail had held no obstacles to his returning. The bridge he had built to traverse the creek cutting across the trail was still solid. He could tell, even with a covering of snow, that it was still straddling the creek on a level plane, with no collapse imminent.

After crossing the bridge, he finally saw some animal sign, both wolf and moose. The wolf tracks had been made next to and over the hoof prints, definitely on the hunt. About two hundred yards from the cabin, they veered off to the left. Denny figured the moose would travel across the frozen lake, hidden from sight on the far side of the low ridge behind his place. He had seen lots of sign there in the past.

Despite the darkness, his weariness, and the nearness of his cabin, Denny responded to his natural curiosity and rode out onto the lake to see what, if anything, had occurred there.

The headlight of his machine revealed a confrontation between ancient adversaries. There was blood on the snow-covered lake, showing attacks and defensive moves had been made.

Denny, studying what was before him, decided things had ended in a stand-off, with moose tracks leading away at a slow, steady pace, judging by the distance between strides. There were small blood splatters amongst the moose tracks, but nothing major. The wolves had moved off in a different direction, blood traces amid their prints showing the bull had made the wolves pay for their attempts to bring him down.

Satisfied with what he had observed, Denny headed around to his home.

Stopped in front of his log cabin, the homesteader shut off the machine's engine, the silence of the winter night in stark contrast to the now silent engine's mechanical noises. It had always been pleasant for Denny, the way sounds in winter were muffled by the blanket of snow covering everything. It made for a more restful time, even though he always remained alert for anything unusual signaling possible danger.

He sat for several minutes on the snow machine, letting the after effects of travel subside. Everything that had happened in the past months seemed far away, now that he was home again.

The invasive cold of winter brought him out of his reverie. Kicking some snow away from his front door, he opened it to find his log home safe and sound. He smiled, seeing a little vole skitter across the floor, disappearing under his bed. He knew there would be a nest under there, but wouldn't disturb it, if possible.

Crossing over to the wood stove, he touched a lit match to the tinder pyramid waiting inside. Dry as bone, it took right off. He quickly added larger pieces from the stack next to the stove.

Once the fire was going well, he closed the stove door, before going back outside to bring in the load of supplies he had brought with him. In a few days he would return to his trailer in Salcha with the large freighter sled, to retrieve all his newly bought equipment, including the solar system and back-up generator.

To hurry up the warming process, Caraway also started a fire in his fireplace. He had almost forgotten to remove the metal cap from the wood stove chimney, but remembered in time to keep from smoking himself out of the cabin. Once the airway was open, he got the fire going.

It was good, having both a fireplace and woodstove. The combination had proven very effective in working against winter's desire to put everything into a deep freeze.

Denny did the one thing he always would when he returned to the homestead, going up on the ridge to spend a moment with his dear wife. It mattered not to Denny that she was long passed now. It was her spirit being there that gave him comfort. He had no doubts that she was content to remain on the homestead.

Going back into the cabin, he melted some snow in the stock pot, then transferred some water into a small pan to boil and made himself a cup of Labrador tea. Leaning back in Gwen's old rocker Denny let the feelings of being home seep into his mind. The was plenty to do tomorrow, but for now, he could relax.

Denny had purchased some meat he rarely ate, but enjoyed when he did. Putting some bacon grease into a cast iron skillet, he put two pork chops in to fry. They started sizzling almost immediately. He poured some frozen peas from their plastic bag into the hot water left in the little sauce pan and, within a short time, had a tasty meal ready. He would take a moose soon enough, but for now, the chops would do just fine.

The next morning, he awoke to what sounded like a single engine plane coming in for a landing on the lake across from his place. He had no idea who it might be, but considered it could be Caroline or Stanley. He stretched and began dressing, but before he was able to leave the cabin and snowshoe over to the lake, Caraway heard the airplane taking off again.

Going outside and climbing the rise, all he saw were several sets of ski tracks showing someone had landed, but changed their mind for some unknown reason, and left again. Denny shrugged, then snowshoed back to the cabin, spending little time pondering who had come and gone so quickly.

After being around other people the whole summer, though he had enjoyed their company for the most part, he was in need of some peace and solitude. He knew having ample time alone was a true necessity for him.

Denny went inside the cabin once again, hanging the bear paw snowshoes on their hooks outside the front door. Now he needed a first cup of morning coffee to restart the day.

Three days later, he rode out the trail to retrieve the rest of his goods from the trailer. It snowed lightly all the way out, and back in the next day, but Denny didn't mind.

Chapter Fourteen

The two people who had landed the Cessna 172 on the frozen lake behind the homestead had no good intentions. They had flown down from Fairbanks to find Denny Caraway. The passenger knew he lived along a tributary of the Salcha River, because Denny, when he had worked for him several years prior, had mentioned where his homestead was located.

The man who had come to find him was no stranger to the Alaskan bush and soon had his pilot flying over the Salcha river until they spotted the cabin and shed about where he figured the homestead would be.

No, Carlton O'Bannion was not there for a friendly visit; he had come to settle the score with Caraway. If Nathan Barker had not died, something O'Bannion had read about in the Fairbanks newspaper, he would have dealt with him, too, unwilling to admit that his own deceitfulness had ruined his life.

The small plane taxied up to the edge of the lake nearest Caraway's cabin, behind the low rise acting as a buffer between the lake and the homestead, and the pilot cut the engine. O'Bannion got out, shotgun in hand, a cold look in his eyes. But, he stopped short, staring at something on the ridge top. The pilot had joined him.

"Who's the woman standing there watching us?" he asked. "I thought you told me this guy Caraway was alone out here."

"He's supposed to be, Matt."

"Then what's she doing there?"

"How the heck do I know? I think we'd better back off though, until I can figure this out."

Climbing back into the plane and cranking it up, they taxied back out onto the lake and were soon winging their way north.

What they had seen, what had run them off, was a woman dressed in a heavy parka, the hood back, her brown hair in two braids. She was holding a big old-fashioned rifle in the crook of her arm. She didn't move or make a sound, but it was obvious she was looking right at them, and it put a stop to their plans. For now, Denny Caraway was still safe, with someone watching over him.

Chapter Fifteen

The winter was a time of healing for Denny. Living the life again, replenishing firewood, keeping the water hole clear in the creek, and hiking through the country was a catharsis for him.

He had taken a fine three-year-old bull, perfect for eating, only a quarter mile from the homestead. Caraway had done his share of hauling in meat from a real distance, so the nearness of this kill was a blessing.

He read, ate, slept, and made repairs to his gear. As the mood struck, he took hikes along the creek and once to a place he never expected to see again. Fueling up the snow machine and carrying extra gas with him, Denny rode to the humble abode he had lived in after Gwen's death, the tiny cabin hidden away in the trees. He had no trouble finding it, but it was buried in snow, and Denny could see the roof had given way.

Standing in front of the snowy ruins, Denny found he was not put into a bad state of mind. The cabin itself held no special meaning for him now. Searching his feelings, the man knew he truly had gotten past his worst time of life. No longer having any reason to be there, Caraway walked out to the snow machine and headed back to his true home.

While some wilderness dwellers had been known to go bushy from being alone too long, despite everything he'd been through, Denny remained solid.

In the middle of March, he needed to replenish his perishables, making a run to Fairbanks necessary. The trail was good, break-up still some time away, so he hitched his freighter sled to the snow machine. The first thing he'd do in Fairbanks would be to visit Caroline and Max.

When Denny arrived at the Barker house, Caroline met him at the door, holding Maxwell in her arms. Caraway was even more pleased to see them than he had anticipated. He had said they were like family to him. Now he knew how true his own words were. Appearing happy to see him, Caroline gave him a kiss on the cheek and invited him in.

They caught up on things, though she did most of the talking. Denny didn't have much to say about himself, except that he kept busy, and the winter had gone easily for him.

Max had grown quickly and was very active, scooting around on the floor, pulling himself up onto his feet, and getting into everything. Caraway noticed the child smiled and laughed a lot, and he was glad to be around the boy again.

Caroline told him she planned to spend the whole first summer season at Burl Lake.

"I'm going to cook the meals and try to keep the clients happy when they're not fishing, though being at the lodge in each other's company will probably be enough to keep them entertained. After all, these people live for fishing. My only concern is having Max in the bush with us, because he's so young and helpless. What do you think?"

Without hesitation, Denny said, "He'll be fine; we'll keep him safe. I think he'll like it."

Caroline smiled and nodded. She knew what Denny's answer would be, but it felt good to hear him say it. The two friends had a nice dinner together, then sat and talked about their ideas and hopes for the lodge, turning in around midnight.

At breakfast, Denny mentioned the curious incident of the light aircraft landing on the frozen lake by his homestead, but taking off again before he'd actually seen it. Caroline told him she knew nothing about it.

After visiting for another hour, Denny said his good-byes, then left to restock what supplies he needed at his homestead before heading south. He had wanted to speak to Everett Tanner about how the winter had gone, but the man was down in Homer visiting friends. It was pretty clear to Denny that Everett had been taking care of things, as he figured he would.

Back in Salcha, Denny went over to the North Star Cafe for a visit with Charlie Brady. Walking into the cafe, he saw Drew was there also.

The three friends sat and visited. Brady asked him how things were going out at the homestead. Denny, picking up on the meaning behind the question said, "Being back on the creek has been good for me, Charlie, better than I expected. There are times when things seem just like they used to be."

Nodding in response, Charlie refilled Caraway's coffee mug.

Denny looked at Drew. "Speaking of the homestead, Drew, you ready to come visit?"

It was as if a light lit up in the young man. "I sure am, Mr. Caraway. Should I go get my gear together? I could meet you at your trailer."

Denny smiled and said, "Sure, Drew. I should be down there in twenty minutes or so."

Denny and Charlie sat a while longer, drinking coffee and talking about Salcha. There had been some development going on, a number of new people moving into the area. But Charlie, with his law enforcement background, could sniff out a bad character, and he thought the new people coming in all seemed fine. "Can't stop things from growing, Denny, even here in Salcha. You might have some company yourself, out on the creek."

Denny stopped, the cup half way to his mouth. He flashed Brady a questioning look, wondering what he meant, until Charlie smiled and said, "Maybe in a hundred years or so."

Caraway didn't find much humor in his joke, saying, "Real cute, Officer Brady."

"I thought so, Mr. Caraway. I'm sure you're safe out there. The influx of folks has helped my business, that's definite."

Denny arrived at his trailer to find Drew sitting on the front steps. His old snow machine had a pack tied to the back of the seat, with a set of small snowshoes strapped on top.

"Well, Drew, you seem ready to go. Help me load up the supplies in the sled, will you?"

In a matter of minutes, the two men were headed out the trail. Since Drew had never been out that far, Denny took it easy, to give the young man a chance to observe the country.

They stopped several times so he could enjoy views Denny thought were worth pausing to see. Drew told Denny he thought it must be great to live so deep in the forest full time.

Denny responded, "It is, Drew, the best life I know."

Arriving at the homestead in the dark, Denny did as he always did, sitting a minute on the machine, savoring the moment of return. Drew had hopped off his machine, but seeing Denny sitting there, he quietly waited until Denny got off his snow machine and opened the front door.

Drew loved the log cabin, taking time to thoroughly examine it. He especially liked that it had both a wood stove and a fireplace. When Denny mentioned Richard Proenneke, Drew gave him a blank look, so Denny told him about the remote homesteader, the beautiful cabin he built, and how he had lived alone for over thirty years on the shore of Twin Lakes. Drew was impressed.

In the week the two men stayed on the homestead together, Drew thoroughly enjoyed doing everything, even breaking out the water hole and bringing in wood. For his part, Caraway was happy to have the young man visit. He was a good person with no bad habits Denny could detect, except for a thundering snore. The first night, Denny frowned and put the pillow over his head to sleep.

In the morning, Denny told Drew there must have been a hungry bear around in the night.

Drew got a serious look on his face, until Denny said, "Yeah, it seemed like the bear was right inside the cabin, growling very loudly."

Drew became self-conscious, realizing what Denny was actually talking about, but the old homesteader told him it was all right; he was only teasing.

After a good breakfast of bacon, eggs, and fry bread, Denny took Drew out to see the lake. They snowshoed up the little rise, because the view was best there. Getting to the top, Denny gently put his left arm out, causing Drew to stop. Drew gave him a quizzical look, until Denny pointed to the ground and said, "This is where Gwen is buried. It's such a beautiful view, I thought she'd like it here."

Drew nodded and remained silent.

The two men had a good time, roaming around or sitting peacefully in the cabin, eating, talking, and playing cribbage. Drew knew how to play, and by the end of the visit, the younger man had won his share of games.

When the time came for Drew to leave, Denny offered to guide him back out, but Drew told him it wasn't necessary. Denny understood the young man wanting to ride out by himself. The trail was good, with no new snow to conceal it, their tracks still visible, so Denny knew he should be all right.

Drew shook Caraway's hand and thanked him for sharing his home.

Before he started up his machine, Drew turned and told Denny he was sure Gwen liked the place she was resting in. "It really is a beautiful view from up there."

Denny nodded in agreement. Drew cranked up his machine and headed towards Salcha. Denny stood until he was out of sight and hearing, before going back inside.

During the visit, Denny had asked Drew if he'd be interested in being the assistant fishing guide at Burl Lake Lodge. Denny had come to know Drew better in the time they spent together. He thought the young Alaskan would be good to have at the lodge. You would have thought Denny had handed him a big gold bar when he offered him the job. Drew accepted enthusiastically.

"I'll get in touch early in June. The lodge will open on June Fifteenth, so we'll have time to work out all the details and get ready for the clients."

Chapter Sixteen

S pring break-up began at the end of April, a bit early for the Salcha River area. Denny had brought in his wheeler from the trailer before break-up had begun, hauling it back to the homestead in his freighter sled.

By the middle of May, there was less snow left than normal. The temperature had already reached the fifties a number of times, also unusual. But Denny, in the years he'd lived there, had learned he could never second guess the weather.

In the first week of June, Denny headed out the trail on his wheeler, his gear packed on the back and front racks, the little ATV trailer hitched up in back. He had bought a molded plastic rifle scabbard in Fairbanks, lined with a soft furry material, and a mount for securing it to the ATV, on the right side behind his leg. There was a padded top to go with it, but Denny decided to leave the top off. The old Winchester lever action fit into the case very snugly. Barring a major accident with the wheeler, it would be secure and easier to get to, with the top unattached.

He arrived at Salcha with no problems. Though the creek cutting across the trail was running fast and high, Denny's log-and-slab bridge was holding strong. A quick inspection of the structure showed a few small repairs were needed, but it was still in good shape.

After a quick stop at Grandpa Elliot's house to let Drew know he was in Salcha, Denny and Drew connected at Charlie's cafe. A week earlier, Drew had already packed what he thought he'd need for working at the lodge. During the summer, Brady would look in on both Drew's house and Denny's trailer, to make sure all was well.

Drew was duly impressed with the Barker house up on Chena Ridge. "Wow," he said, "what a big, beautiful cabin. I mean, it's a house, of course, but it still feels like a cabin, only, uh, big."

Caroline came to the door. Denny was surprised to see Max standing by her side, holding onto her hand.

"Drew, this is Caroline Barker, and this little man is Max, her son, who wasn't standing last time I saw him."

"And walking too," added Caroline.

"And walking, too." Caraway couldn't help but flash a big smile.

"Caroline, this is Drew, the young man I told you about."

Caroline smiled and gave Drew a hug. His face got red at the unexpected show of affection.

They went inside and relaxed for a while, drinking coffee and discussing the coming season. They'd have to fly in all the food and other supplies and get the generator up and running for the kitchen appliances and the freezer. Then they could open up the place and get everything arranged.

Caroline had a little surprise for Denny, and Drew as well. She came out of a back room with a cotton canvas shirt, khaki in color, and told the boys they would wear them at the lodge. "There will be three for each of us."

Denny gave her a quizzical look, until she held up the shirt, and he saw over the breast pocket the embroidered words: "Burl Lake Fishing Lodge," in large, green letters. A leaping trout with a fishing line coming from its mouth was embroidered in blue above the lettering. Denny smiled and shook his head.

Drew spoke up, "The shirt is really great, Miss Barker. Very professional looking. Thanks!"

Denny gave Drew a quick look, shrugged, and told Caroline he thought they'd be good shirts for outdoor work.

An hour later, they had loaded everything up in Nathan's old Chevy Suburban and driven to the airport to meet Stanley who was waiting with the Otter. Soon they were winging their way to Burl Lake. Max wasn't scared. He was too busy looking out the window, making all sorts of excited noises.

Drew was quiet, watching the country slip by beneath them. He was thinking forward to what summer might hold, and couldn't wait to get started.

The big Otter, at Stanley's deft touch, came in for a smooth landing, sliding gently up to the dock. Drew stepped out and stood looking at the lodge, the other buildings, and the surrounding country. All he could say was, "Wow!"

Once all their gear was unloaded onto the dock, Stanley took his leave. He had business of his own, but in three days he would bring out the first clients.

"Well," Denny said, once all the gear was stowed in the lodge and the bunk room where he and Drew would reside, "let's get started. We've got plenty to do."

Chapter Seventeen

The first season at Burl Lake Lodge had wound down, and the last satisfied fishermen returned home. Now, Denny, Drew, and Caroline were putting the place into winter mode.

Things had gone well for Denny, whose concerns about dealing with people had been dispelled once the first clients came in. As Nathan had wanted, the clients were a very select group, chosen by Caroline for their serious love of fishing and the outdoors. The application for fishing at Burl Lake was oriented towards that. Denny found he related easily to all of them. At times it was like having friends come visit. He'd learned a lot about fly fishing, also. While he had previously considered fly fishing a "snooty" hobby, he saw it differently now, seeing how much finesse and expertise it required.

Virtually all the clients were experienced, knowledgeable fly fishermen. One couple had grumbled about having to keep what fish they caught. They were staunch supporters of catch and release, a type of fishing Denny never appreciated, being strictly a catch-and-eat fisherman. But they finally had accepted the lodge's rule about keeping what you caught, which had been in the initial description of the guide service. They would eat some of the fresh fish they caught at the lodge, and any they didn't want to eat or ship home frozen, would be donated to a kitchen in Fairbanks for the needy, after the season was over.

Marcel Durier had even given Denny a fine rod and reel as a thank you for making the visit a memorable one and gave Denny a few lessons before returning home to France.

Gifting him the handmade rod and precision reel might have had something to do with Denny keeping a big black bear from potentially mauling the man, while they were fishing in a tight area on Bent Birch Creek.

Getting between the fisherman and the troublesome animal, Denny had confronted the bear, the old Winchester at the ready, letting the bruin know the aggressive attitude he arrived with would not be tolerated. The blackie took some convincing, but Denny's firm stance and voice had the same effect on the bear it'd had on bad actors in the past, aggressive animals and humans both.

After the bear had reluctantly left, Denny turned to find the client standing there smiling.

The Frenchman said, "Miss Barker told me you were a reliable man to have in the bush for a guide, Mr. Caraway, an experienced woodsman, and she certainly wasn't kidding. I have the feeling this wasn't the first bear you've had to deal with."

Denny gave a little shrug of his shoulders and responded, "Sometimes they take a little extra convincing to see the error of their ways. This one was smart enough to finally get my point."

"I had heard, Mr. Caraway, that black bears are usually no problem, preferring to run away rather than make trouble. But, this one apparently hadn't been informed of how he should behave."

"My experience has taught me you can never tell what a bear may do, Mr. Durier, no matter which kind it is."

"Well, shall we do a little more fishing here?"

"Actually, it might be better to find a location somewhere else on the lake. If he comes back, I might not be able to change his mind a second time."

The two men traveled to a different part of the lake and continued fishing. The bear episode had strengthened the bond between them, as only such a situation might. All in all, it ended up being a very satisfying day for them both.

Denny's feeling that Drew would be a welcome addition to the lodge had proven to be right. Drew was a nice, polite young man. He knew when to speak and when to listen, which was appreciated. He seemed to have an instinct for acting appropriately with each client.

The young man had been fishing in Alaska his whole life. His enthusiasm at being out in the bush had proven contagious. Drew received a number of compliments and several nice tips for the way he made the fishing more enjoyable for the clients. He also seemed to have a gut sense for finding good fishing sites. One of the clients, who wanted to catch a big northern pike, came back grinning from ear to ear. He said to Denny, when he returned to the lodge, "It's not as big as some of the muskies and northerns I've caught up in Minnesota and Michigan, but this fish gave me as good a fight as I've had anywhere. Must be something in this Alaska water, eh?" He let out a loud guffaw, then another, causing Denny to smile openly.

Caroline had cornered Caraway the morning before the first fisherman arrived and told him to make sure to smile for the clients. "Make sure they can see it when you do, Denny."

Now, the season over, the lodge was being shut down until next summer. Drew was in the kitchen, making sure any foods that could be affected by the freezing temperatures of winter had all been removed, to be taken over to Charlie Brady's North Star Cafe. Charlie and Denny had worked out a deal. Any food left at the end of the fishing season, Charlie could use at the cafe, sold to him at a fair price.

Charlie had come out for three days to fish, as Denny had invited him to do. One of the boats was given to him to go anywhere on the lake he chose. Charlie had a fine time and caught several really nice lake trout. It was good for him to take a break from the cafe, which he rarely did. He was an avid outdoorsman, and this was just what he needed. As for Caraway, he was glad to be able to do something for his good friend.

There were three clients at the time Charlie arrived. While he was there, in the evenings they all sat around the main room and chewed the fat. Charlie and Denny talked about hunting and fishing in Alaska, and the clients responded with their own experiences. The feeling of being with good friends, rather than people who have met briefly, was strong. Caroline enjoyed listening to the men talk. She could have told of a few adventures herself. At one point, she and Denny made eye contact as Charlie was telling a story from his days as a wildlife officer. The look passing between them affirmed this was one of those perfect moments.

Caroline was in charge of meals, and she had made sure there was plenty of Alaska food besides the fresh fish the fishermen themselves provided. There were king crab legs, dungeness crab, and shrimp, as well as moose. The fishermen found the meals entertaining and delicious.

Drew was grateful to Denny for giving him the job at the lodge. He loved Burl Lake, located as it was in the heart of pristine wilderness. He told Denny he thought the country around the lake must be like all of Alaska once was, before so many people had come north. By summer's end, though, he was glad to be going back to his house in Salcha, as much as Denny was looking forward to returning to his homestead.

Drew, Denny, and Caroline would fly out in the Otter with Stanley, who had done a great job ferrying the clients in and out to Burl Lake. All the fishermen enjoyed his descriptive commentary of Alaska as they flew from Fairbanks to the lodge.

Caroline went to the lodge's back room and brought out her son Max, where he had been napping. He had handled living at the lodge well that summer and had given the clients more than a few amusing moments. He was a natural clown and loved the attention.

Though very young, it was amazing how aware he was of the wild country they were in. He seemed to know it was a potentially dangerous place, never straying very far from the lodge or his mom. But, neither did he seem afraid, constantly interested in everything around him. Denny and Caroline took him for a few walks during the brief moments they had without clients to deal with. Secure in their company, Max took in everything around him, absorbing the sights, sounds, and smells. He seemed quite at home, a fact that impressed Denny.

There was one moment that had Denny momentarily worried. He came out from the supply room to see Max, alone, looking at a porcupine only a few feet away, his quills totally flared out, with its back to the boy. Denny slowly walked over and gently took his hand. Max grabbed it as tightly as he could, a serious look on his face. He seemed to know this was a creature you shouldn't mess with. How he knew, Denny wasn't sure, since Max had never seen one before. Denny decided he was a naturally skookum child. Max looked up at Caraway, and an understanding passed between them about the scary looking animal. Max tugged on Denny's hand, and they walked away into the lodge.

Denny told Caroline what had transpired, and she shook her head.

"He's a natural, isn't he Denny? Just like you."

"Well, like his grandfather and the same as my grandpa was, C. But I was no natural; I had a lot to learn."

"Oh, poo, you just needed to be in the right situations to bring out what was already in you."

A little chill went down Denny's back when Caroline said "Oh, poo." It had been one of Gwen's favorite little remarks whenever she disagreed with something Caraway had said.

Denny's shiver caused Caroline to gave him a questioning look. He only smiled and shook his head.

The four of them were sorry to leave the lodge. They all loved it there, the old homesteader, the woman, her son, and the young man, all true Alaskans sharing the joy of being in the best place they knew.

As they sat together, awaiting Stanley's arrival, Caroline asked Denny a very intimate question, one she would not have asked if she didn't know him as well as she did.

"Denny?"

"Yes C, what's up?"

"May I ask you something personal and not disturb you?"

"Silly question. What do you want to know?"

"I need to know if you are okay now about Gwen's passing, and don't feel guilty that she lived remote with you, far from help. I know you're in no way to blame, but I want to be sure you know, too."

Denny was quiet for a long minute, searching his mind and heart for a way to explain to her how he felt.

"There was a time, after she'd first died, when I was in my dark times in the woods, that I completely blamed myself. At one point I stopped eating, bent on getting rid of the pain I felt from wanting the chance to be with her again. But the desire in me to live was too strong, and I continued to survive and struggle with my grief.

"I later came to realize why things had happened the way they did. I understood I was meant to be a solitary man, living my life in the bush as I had done for years. But I gave in to feelings of loneliness. I thought having Gwen with me on the homestead would be a good thing, a natural part of it, and a reason to be happy.

"What I had actually done was to go against my destiny. It changed everything. And I truly believe she died because I had changed the way things were meant to be, for me and for her. I will always believe it to be true, but have accepted there was no way of knowing and will cherish the time we did have together. I know it made her happy, too."

A wave of emotion overcame Denny, not having spoken of Gwen and his feelings like this before. He walked out of the lodge and wandered along the lake until he had collected himself. As he walked back to the front porch, Stanley arrived. He waved to the pilot and went into the lodge to gather the gear. Denny and Drew busied themselves with loading the plane. Caroline came up to Denny and apologized for upsetting him. But Denny assured her he was glad to tell someone how he felt.

Without thinking, out of the great affection he felt, Caraway gave her a tight hug. There was a spark between them. Denny was hesitant to let her go, not wanting to look her in the eyes, afraid of what he might see there. Caroline, sensing the way he was feeling, slipped gently away without looking directly at him. But, the feelings didn't leave them for some time.

Half an hour later, Denny and Drew had loaded up the remaining personal items, and they departed, leaving the lodge to deal with winter's burden. The structures had proven their sturdiness the previous year, so winter damage was not a worry, even though the snow loads could be great in that part of Alaska.

The flight went smoothly, the good friends sitting without much talking, sharing the time. Max again enjoyed the flight over the wild terrain below, looking out the windows intently.

It had been a good season, hopefully the first of many to come.

Chapter Eighteen

Caraway spent several days in Fairbanks, preparing for his return to the homestead, but first he helped Caroline open up the house again.

Tanner had not returned yet from his summer surveying job. The arrangement Caroline had made with Nathan's former surveyor had worked out well. He was a good man, and she had appreciated having him around to help out. For his part, Tanner was glad to have winter work and a nice place to live. Caroline had decided to let him start working and living at the house well in advance of winter, as soon as he was done surveying. Denny was fine with his being there, knowing he was a totally trustworthy man.

With Caroline and Max settled back in, Denny was ready to go home. He spent the night at the house, but left very early in the morning, before anyone was up. He left a note, saying he'd get in touch before summer.

Neither of them had made any mention of the moment between them on that last day at the lodge, which was a relief to Caraway.

Driving downtown to pick up some supplies, he saw Robert Pete in his old Jeep pick-up and hailed him. The two men parked and greeted each other.

Robert said he had found work in town at a building supply store.

"I'd prefer to work outside, but it's steady and pays the bills. I got married, you know."

Denny congratulated his friend, and Robert asked if he'd like to meet his new wife. Caraway couldn't refuse. So, they drove over to Robert's little home. His wife turned out to be a petite young woman from Selawik, named Evie. She was pretty and seemed very happy.

Robert grinned and said, "She's a good cook and knows how to sew traditional clothing. She does everything a good wife should do."

His wife giggled.

"Yes," Robert said with a big grin, "I'm a very lucky man."

Denny sat and visited with Robert for a while, but he had to get back to buying the supplies he needed. He told Robert he hadn't been to his homestead all summer, and the Native man understood his desire to get back, but he wanted to do something for Denny.

"So, Mr. Caraway, do you have anyone to keep you company at your place?"

"No, Robert, I'm on my own out there."

"Well, we can fix that for you. Come outside with me."

Caraway followed him to the back of the house, where there were half a dozen wooden dog kennels. Robert went to one, squatted down, and pulled out a female dog. To Denny, it looked like just a mutt.

Robert said, "This dog is a good one, always ready to pull, with lots of energy. I watch dogs for mushers sometimes, if they're pregnant, or if they just don't want to keep them around the other dogs. I always find homes for the pups when they're old enough. I've got one right here I know would be perfect for you."

Then Robert pulled out one of the female's pups, about eight weeks old. It was a chunky little thing, mostly white with a half-brown head, including one ear, and a brown tip on its tail. Denny couldn't figure out what kind of dog it was, but he thought it was a nice pup. He asked Robert what breed he thought it was. He noticed it was a male, which was fine with him.

"Well, I know it's one part Siberian, one part regular poodle, and something else, I don't know what for sure. I know one of the males, and he's a good dog. I think a dog would be good for you, and I'd like to give you this one, for a friend. You could train it to carry a pack while you're out snowshoeing, and it could travel on the trail with you."

Denny hadn't considered having another dog since he'd lost his first one to a couple of coyotes years back at his first homestead. He vowed he would never have another dog, not wanting to lose it, too. But a lot had happened since then, and the idea now appealed to him.

"You know Robert, I think I will take it. Might be nice having a dog around, as long as it behaves. Is it on regular food yet?"

"Yep, been weaned for about a week now. It's good you'll take him. Makes me happy."

So, Denny had another dog. He said good-bye to the Petes and carried the pup to his truck in a box Robert had put it in. Stopping at a store, he bought some puppy chow and two bowls for the pup, which he hadn't named yet.

Evie had given him some smoked salmon for the drive, which was delicious.

"Robert is indeed a lucky man," Denny thought to himself, as he headed south to Salcha.

Back in Salcha, except for having the puppy, which Charlie Brady thought was a good Alaska dog, examining it while Denny ate his regular meal of burger and fries, the routine Caraway went through was the same as always. He spent the night in his trailer, the pup in the little box on the floor by the bed. It cried until he hung his arm down into the box, where the dog snuggled up against it.

In the morning, he loaded up the little trailer, put some supplies and his trail gear on the wheeler's racks and headed out the trail. At first, he didn't know the best way to carry the pup. He thought of strapping the box onto a rack, but the rough trail might give the little dog quite a jostling. Finally, he tucked the dog into his jacket, strapping his gun belt on the outside, so he couldn't slip out the bottom. The little guy seemed quite content to be tucked in against his human. Warming up the wheeler, Denny bent his head down and told the pup they were going to his new home, and everything would be fine. The dog twisted his head around and gave Denny's chin a little lick, as if to tell him he was ready to go. Shifting the wheeler into gear, Denny headed out to the trailhead toward home.

Caraway stopped twice to let the pup do his business and sniff around. The little mutt seemed quite serious about checking out all the new scents. Denny allowed him some time to acquaint himself with the land.

Coming to the bridged creek, the dog got very excited looking at the water running by under the bridge. Denny kept an eye on the pup, thinking it might try to jump in, but it didn't.

The cabin finally came into view. Denny was pleased, as always, to see it. He saw there were bear claw marks on the door framing. The bruin wanted in, but the solidly built cabin kept the marauder out.

Setting the pup down, Denny kept an eye on it while unloading the trailer and ATV. Until the dog was old enough to deal with life in the woods, he'd have to keep it safe.

After putting everything away, Denny put down a bowl of puppy food and one full of water. He whistled, and the pup came waddling in. Putting his two front paws on Denny's boot, the dog stood looking up at him. Caraway picked him up and placed him in front of the food bowl. The little dog took one sniff, shoved his muzzle into the kibble and started eating, not stopping until there was nothing left. Denny planned on slowly mixing moose meat and fish into the dog's food until the bag of kibble was gone, after which, the dog would eat whatever meat or fish Denny had on hand.

Denny began cooking a stew for dinner, using fresh onions and potatoes, canned green beans, and a jar of moose meat from the cache. Taking a small piece of meat, he offered it to the dog, who took one sniff and snatched the meat from Caraway's fingers. He looked at Denny, obviously wanting more. Denny gave him another little piece, which he also grabbed and swallowed in an instant.

"Well, you'll be no trouble to feed, you little rip. Hey, I'll call you Rip. Good as any other name, right?"

The pup stood looking at Denny, waiting for another piece of meat, but didn't get any more. Rip walked over to the little braided rug by the side of Denny's bed and, turning around several times, plopped down, yawned, and fell asleep.

Denny thought, "*Like you've always lived here.*"

Walking quietly out of the cabin, Caraway went up the little slope, and stood talking to Gwen, where she lay in the ground between the two birches. He described the summer's events, how things were for him, and the pup.

"I wish you were here to enjoy the little dickens. I think he'll be good to have out here. I know you'd like him, too."

Right after he spoke, a chickadee landed on a branch directly above his head and began chirping. After listening to the bird's message a while, he walked back to the cabin.

Going in, he saw the pup standing just inside the door. Denny patted him on the head, and Rip went back to the rug, lay down again, and fell right to sleep. Denny stirred the stew, made a cup of tea, and sat peacefully at the table. The pup began making little yips in his sleep. Denny wondered what he might be dreaming.

As fall slipped away and winter came in, Denny felt as if he had never left his homestead. He had regained the peace and contentment of his chosen home and the perfection of his life there. He'd come full circle, from his earlier homesteading life alone, to Gwen living with him, and now back to the way he was meant to be, in his mind, a solitary man in paradise.

Rip grew quickly. He was becoming a sturdy dog, with a thick curly coat of hair. He easily learned whatever Denny wanted to teach him, and had figured some things out by instinct and with his innate intelligence.

Denny was impressed one day, when they came across a porcupine while hiking through the forest, looking for possible firewood trees. Some dogs had to get a muzzle full of quills to learn about porkies the hard way, and some dogs never learned. Rip never got close enough for the prickly animal to shake his quills at him. He knew better from the get-go.

After the day's chores were done, Denny would play with Rip, throwing sticks for him and wrestling around. The two of them were already taking hikes through the woods, and Rip had become familiar with everything there.

The freezing temperatures didn't seem to bother him, and he loved the first snowfall, running around, snapping at the falling snow, and rolling in it, until Denny couldn't help but laugh at his antics. Robert was right, Rip was good to have around.

During the winter, on several occasions, they heard wolves howling, once quite close by.

Rip would stand by the cabin door, his head turned towards Denny. He'd whine quietly until Denny would put on his parka and hat and go out with him to listen. Rip would join in the singing, but he was still young, and his voice hadn't come of age yet.

The first time Rip heard the wolves call, Denny went outside with him, and the young dog began to run towards the sound, but Caraway called him back. Rip stood looking towards the sound and back at Denny several times, before returning to sit at his feet. He seemed resigned to stay with his human. The dog whined quietly, with longing. Denny roughed Rip's head with his gloved hand. Rip looked up at him and smiled a dog smile.

Chapter Nineteen

The second season at Burl Lake had been as close to perfect as anything in life can be. The weather was excellent all summer, and the bugs were in low numbers. The fish were biting on whatever the fishermen tossed at them.

There were no problems with clients. They had all been very happy with their experiences at the lodge. Caroline had booked more fishermen than last season, twenty-eight in all, but there had been no problem in handling them. The last fishermen of the summer were packing their gear, their time at the lodge almost over. They would be flying out in the morning.

Drew had again been a great asset. Everyone liked him as in the first season, with his easy-going nature, and respectful, polite manner. After several clients remarked on Drew's ability to locate fish, Denny had asked him about it. Drew smiled and told Denny there were places on the lake "that just smell like fish."

The daughter of Caroline's best friend, Angela, had graduated from chef's school in Anchorage, before the season had begun. Her specialty was seafood, but she knew how to cook anything she put her talents to. Caroline had asked her if she would like to come to Burl Lake Lodge for the season, to get some on-the-job experience. Though she had originally planned to look for employment in the Lower Forty-Eight, she decided to take the job at the lodge, much to everyone's delight. Becka was a terrific chef, and everything she cooked tasted wonderful. She would even go collect natural greens to use in the meals. Caroline knew it was going to be a special time at the lake.

Max was a real hoot, and the clients enjoyed his antics. The boy was obviously a very intelligent toddler. He had a grasp of the abstract and his mother's wry wit. More than once he said something to a client that didn't register as a funny comment immediately, especially coming from a child, but it would come to the person a few moments later, eliciting a smile and shake of the head.

Denny and Max were close, the child staying near Caraway whenever he could. Though he wasn't allowed to go out with Denny or Drew if they were guiding, Denny would take him out in the early evenings while he fished off the dock. Though too young to fish himself, he paid close attention to everything Denny did.

The day Denny had shown up with Rip at the Barker house, Caroline was delighted. She called him, and he seemed to be coming toward her, but instead, he trotted past and went up to Max and stood there, inches from the boy. Max let out an excited squeal and wrapped his arms around the young dog's neck. Rip made little whining noises, delighted to have the child holding on to him. The two became immediate friends.

"Denny," Caroline said, as they both stood watching the boy and dog together, "it looks like we've been upstaged."

During their flight out to the lake, it had taken a few minutes before Rip settled down in the plane. He barked and yowled, Maxwell laughing all the while.

Rip was accepted by everyone at the lodge. He was a well-mannered dog, especially with strangers. He only growled a warning once when a fisherman thoughtlessly teased him with the end of his rod, flicking it at Rip's nose. But Denny quietly told Rip to go lie down, and he did. Caraway gave the fisherman a slightly irritated look, and the fisherman apologized. Denny forced himself to crack a smile, telling the man it was all right, no harm done.

Caroline later told Denny she was proud of him for having such good self-control.

Denny assumed a deep scowl and told her it would be best if it didn't happen again. He winked at Caroline and walked away.

She thought to herself, "*Denny Caraway winking, that's a new one on me.*"

As Caroline was headed to the kitchen to help Becka put everything in order, Drew came over and told Caroline she had a call. Caroline said hello into the satellite phone, and a man who introduced himself as Jerry Easton told her he wanted to come fishing at the lodge. Caroline told him the season was over, but she would be happy to book him in for next year.

"I'm sorry to hear it," the man replied. "Is there any chance I could come out and look things over? I'm in Anchorage right now, and I have a friend with an airplane. I could be out tomorrow."

"You could view our website. It has all the information you need, including a number of images of the lodge."

"Well, I suppose that would be okay, but I'd love to see the place in the flesh, so to speak. I could come out tomorrow, spend an hour or so and make a final decision. I could bring a friend next year, so you would have two paying customers. All I'd need is the lake's location for my friend to fly me there."

Caroline sighed and agreed to let Mr. Easton come out for a look-see. She wasn't pleased with his pushy attitude, but an hour wouldn't interfere with anything. She gave him the GPS coordinates for the pilot and signed off. One of the remaining clients came over to talk, and Caroline dismissed the call from her mind.

Chapter Twenty

Carlton O'Bannion set the phone down and smiled. It was not a pleasant smile. His time for revenge seemed near.

He was still obsessed with getting back at the person he blamed for the bad turn his life had taken. He refused to believe it was his own fault he had basically lost everything. He had never reopened his guide business, after spending ninety days at the Fairbanks Correctional Center.

His attempts to make a new start had not gone well. He wasn't capable of being a decent man, and his attitude and behavior saw the end of a number of money-making schemes. The last one he tried, a firewood business, had folded because, not only was he shorting people on wood, he was cutting trees down on state land illegally. He was given a fine and a stern warning. Of course, somehow it was Denny Caraway who had caused this, too.

He had heard about Nathan Barker's death in the Fairbanks paper, and anyone who knew O'Bannion would think he would be pleased at the news, Barker being the other person besides Denny he held responsible for his woes. But he wasn't; he wanted to exact punishment on the both of them himself, but the Cape buffalo that had brought Barker down had robbed him of the opportunity. Now, Denny Caraway was the sole object of his hatred.

O'Bannion's pilot and henchman, Matt, had come over earlier that morning with a page torn from the back of an outdoor magazine containing an ad for Burl Lake Lodge. Seeing Denny Caraway's name listed as the owner, a surge of emotion ran through Carlton O'Bannion. He felt his opportunity had arrived. Now he knew where to find his nemesis.

"Matt, let's take a run out to the airport and get your Cessna set to fly tomorrow. We're headed to Burl Lake."

"But, we don't know how many people are out there. You sure this is a good idea? Remember the woman we saw out at Caraway's place? We weren't expecting her. I'm fine with helping you settle the score with your buddy Caraway, but no one else."

"Going soft on me now that I've finally got a chance for some payback? Maybe I'll get someone else to help me, and you can go to hell!"

O'Bannion's face was now as red as his big, unkempt beard, his anger obvious.

Matt swallowed hard, knowing how the man got when he was angry. "Okay, Carlton, we'll go, but I have a bad feeling about this."

"I don't give a damn how you feel. Let's get out to the airport. I want to leave in the morning, early."

Chapter Twenty One

The last of the clients had been picked up, along with Becka, and flown back to Fairbanks to catch their flights home. They regretted leaving this beautiful place, where they had spent a wonderful week, and vowed to return. Two of them had actually put deposits down for the next season. It seemed as if Burl Lake Lodge's success was assured.

Caroline, Denny, Drew, and little Max sat in the lodge, after eating a breakfast feast. It was pleasant not having to attend to clients for a change. After eating, they sat discussing what went well and a few things needing improvement.

Denny offered Drew a permanent position at better pay, which put an ear-to-ear grin on the young man's face. He expressed his gratitude and told Caroline and Denny he couldn't think of a better way to earn a living.

Drew said, "As great a job as this is, I should be paying you for letting me be here."

Denny put on a stern face and told Drew it could be arranged, but Drew kept smiling.

Drew had let his beard grow out over the summer, and now he looked like a younger version of Caraway, both of them wearing the lodge shirts and Carhartt pants. Caroline teased him, saying he could pass for Denny's younger brother. Drew didn't mind.

Rip began barking, looking behind the lodge. In a moment, the three of them heard a familiar sound coming closer. It was the drone of a single-engine airplane flying overhead.

Walking to the door, Drew told the others there was a small plane headed to the other side of the lake. But instead of coming around to fly back into the wind, the aircraft landed across the lake, near where Frank Clay's camp had been.

Caroline spoke, "It must be Mr. Easton, coming to see the lodge." She put a sleepy Maxwell down for a nap, so she could converse with Mr. Easton when he arrived.

Drew said, "I guess they somehow missed seeing the lodge as they flew over."

Denny thought it was a little odd, but he asked Drew to go over in one of the boats and either tell them to taxi to the lodge, or run them back in the boat. After Drew left, Caroline and Denny went outside to discuss the boat house Denny wanted to build for winter.

Deep in discussion, they both looked up when they heard a loud boom coming from across the lake. Denny immediately knew it was a gunshot blast, probably a rifle. Rip began barking and growling, pacing back and forth on the shore.

Denny ran into the lodge and grabbed the set of binoculars sitting near the front door on a shelf. Looking towards the other side of the lake, he saw Drew's boat apparently just sitting on the water. He couldn't see Drew in the boat, but he did see what appeared to be two men in the plane, though it was too far away to see any clear details. A moment later the Cessna's engine started up.

Caraway went into the bunkhouse and came back out with his rifle. He looked at Caroline, who had a frightened look on her face.

"Caroline, go into the lodge and wait for me."

Jumping into another boat, he was soon tearing across the lake at top speed. The Cessna was already lifting off from the lake's surface and was out of sight before Denny could get to Drew's boat.

When Denny cut the motor and bumped up against Drew's boat, what he saw horrified him.

Drew was lying in the bottom of the boat, clutching at his chest, a large pool of blood spreading beneath him. He stared wide-eyed at Caraway, a stunned look on his face, blood running from his mouth.

Leaping into the boat with him, Denny restarted the motor and headed straight back to the lodge, throttle wide open.

He yelled above the noise of the outboard, "Hang on, Drew, hang on!"

Denny brought the boat up against the dock and tied it off. Caroline was standing there, waiting. She put her hand to her mouth, her eyes showing the shock running through her, seeing what the boat contained. Denny lifted Drew onto the dock, laying him down carefully.

"C, get on the satellite phone, and call the troopers. Tell them we have someone with a gunshot wound. Hurry!"

Terrified, she ran into the lodge. After calling, she checked on Max. Fortunately, he was still asleep. Going to the kitchen, she grabbed a clean dishtowel and ran back out to the dock. She was going to give it to Denny to press against the wound and try to stop the bleeding. But seeing Denny squatting by Drew, motionless, head hanging down, made her realize it was no longer necessary.

Caraway lifted his head, and the expression on his face and in his eyes stopped her. She had never seen such a cold, hard look before, even from Caraway.

"Oh, Denny!"

When she had gone to the lodge, Denny remained kneeling next to Drew, telling him help was coming. Drew tried to say something, in a weak voice. Denny leaned over, to better hear what his young friend was trying to say. Drew spoke into Denny's ear, before going silent.

He had only spoken a few words to Caraway, but they made Denny's gut tighten and his heart go cold.

Caraway put a hand up as a sign for Caroline to be still. After washing his hands in the lake, he walked into the lodge bringing Caroline with him, and called the State Troopers himself on the satellite phone, telling them in detail what had happened. He said to be on the lookout for a small plane coming from the direction of Burl Lake. He didn't know the numbers on the plane, but it was white with red markings. He was sure there were two men in the plane, but couldn't tell them anything else, except Drew was dead. He then signed off.

Denny went back outside with a blanket, which he used to cover Drew's motionless body. He and Caroline went back into the lodge and waited. A while later, Denny heard the troopers flying in, and he met the officers at the dock. He told them what had happened, repeating what he had said on the phone.

One of the troopers, the older one, noticed the look in Caraway's eyes. He knew there was something Denny wasn't saying, something he was holding back. He walked up close to Denny and asked him, "Are you sure there's nothing else you can tell me to help us find whoever was responsible for this?"

He was looking into Caraway's eyes as he asked the question, but there wasn't even a flicker there, nothing the trooper could detect.

All Denny said was, "No."

After the officers took photographs and blood samples from the boat and the dock, Denny took them over to where Drew had been shot, to investigate.

The troopers had been thorough. When finished, they wanted Denny and Caroline to come back to Fairbanks with them, but Denny said they'd be fine. The lodge needed to be closed down, and they would fly out after they were done. The officer who had talked to Denny offered to stay behind with them, but Caraway declined, saying, "I doubt the killers will come back, and I can handle it if they do."

Looking at Caraway, the trooper had no doubt he could take care of things, even though his law enforcement training told him to stay. The officer nodded his agreement. He and his partner loaded Drew's body, now in a body bag, onto the plane. Denny agreed to come by the office in Fairbanks to make out a statement in a few days, and the officers flew out with their tragic cargo.

Denny and Caroline went into the lodge, where Caroline sat and cried, Max sitting with a worried look on his little face, upset by her sorrow. Rip came up to Denny for reassurance, but receiving none, he went and lay down on the porch.

Wanting to do something to break Caroline out of the frame of mind she was in, Denny said, "Caroline, I'm going to start shutting things down now. Call Stanley, and ask him if he can come out tomorrow around noon to pick us up, okay?"

"Of course, Denny, then I'll come help you."

Denny nodded and went outside to do what needed to be done. Before starting all the chores necessary to ready the lodge for winter, he took a mop and bucket to clean off the dock. Caroline came out while he was washing the planks, saw the pink-stained water running off, and went back to the lodge.

Denny was about to wash out the boat Drew had been shot in. But as he stood looking at the pool of blood in its bottom, he knew what he had to do. He removed the motor, tied the boat to another, and ran it out to the middle of the lake. Swinging the axe he had brought, Denny made a half dozen gashes in the bottom of the boat before stepping back into the other and untying the tow rope. He stayed there until the boat had sunk completely out of sight, located the first boat he had come over in, tied it to the boat he now drove, and returned to the lodge.

Caroline was waiting on the dock with Max. She gave Denny a bittersweet smile, and they walked back to the lodge together.

Denny was working on autopilot, going through the motions of getting things done, but his mind was elsewhere, stuck on the words Drew had managed to whisper to him before dying. They were what had turned Caraway's heart into a piece of cold iron, the words he hadn't told the troopers about. Drew had said, "Red beard."

Chapter Twenty Two

The Cessna 172 was flying low, the nervous pilot trying to stay out of the normal range of vision of other planes in the area. He said, "I knew this wasn't going to go right, I knew it."

"Can't change it now, Matt. Let it go, and focus. I want you to land on the lake I told you about. Just get me there, and we're home free. Afterwards, we're through."

"Jesus, O'Bannion, you shot the wrong guy, probably someone who didn't even know who you are! Doesn't it bother you? You're right, we are through. I've done your dirt for you before, but this was too much."

"Long as you keep your mouth shut, you're fine. Remember, you're as much involved as I am. If I get busted, so do you. Besides, nobody saw us. We were up and gone before the guy headed towards us got to the boat, you understand?"

"Oh, I get it, I get it. There's the lake up ahead. You sure nobody's around there?"

"Of course I'm sure. It's on a piece of homestead land that belongs to me, and nobody goes there. Just land the damn plane."

Matt put the Cessna down. If the lake had been any smaller, it would have been a touchy piece of water to land on. As it was, there was little room left and a short taxi to where Carlton wanted to be let off.

After pulling his pack and rifle from the plane, he reminded Matt to keep quiet. Giving him a cold look, O'Bannion growled, "That way, we're both okay."

He shut the side door and waded to shore, watching as the plane headed out onto the lake, turned into the wind, and took off.

Flying over where O'Bannion stood, Matt didn't look his way. He was busy trying to decide where he was going after he got back to his mooring. Wherever it was going to be was fine, as long as it was far away from Carlton O'Bannion.

Walking away from the water into the woods, O'Bannion pulled spruce boughs off an ATV hidden there and strapped his pack onto the rear rack. Walking further into the woods, he dug a narrow, shallow hole in the ground, laid the rifle in it after wiping it down, and covered it up.

Returning to the wheeler, he started it and rode through the trees, turning onto a trail leading to the small cabin he would stay in for a few days. At the right time, he'd carry out the rest of his plan.

Mistaking the guy at Burl Lake for Denny Caraway had drained him of any desire to continue his vendetta, at least for now. He figured Caraway must have known the man he had shot, an employee or maybe even a friend; so, at least there was some small satisfaction for him.

Chapter Twenty Three

Denny and Caroline managed to get the lodge shut down for winter. In the morning, Stanley would come to fly them back to Fairbanks. This time, they wouldn't regret leaving Burl Lake.

That evening was a somber one, with little talk, a light meal, and early to bed. Max had settled down and seemed to be fine.

Caroline remarked to Denny about Max playing happily with his toys on the floor, saying she wished she still had the innocence of childhood.

Denny told her he didn't think there was any innocence left, after what had happened to Drew.

Caroline tried to find a positive response to Caraway's dark remark, but couldn't think of anything to say.

Denny did though: "But, we've got to move on, Caroline, and continue our lives. We'll open the lodge again next June. I'll find someone to help us work the place. It's all we can do."

Caroline nodded her head slowly then took Max to bed.

Denny sat alone in the main lodge room for a while. He kept running two words over and over in his mind. "*Red beard, red beard.*"

Despite the sorrow he was feeling, there was a hard place inside him, which would enable Caraway to do what needed to be done. He didn't consider consequences, because he had no other choice. There was no right or wrong, only what was necessary.

Tired of thinking things through, rising wearily from the overstuffed chair, he went to the bunkhouse, lay down, and slowly drifted off.

Rip had followed him in, and sat next to the bed for a while, his chin on the edge of the bunk, watching Denny until he fell asleep. Only then did the dog lie down. His day was now over, and he closed his eyes to sleep, accepting things as a dog must. Tomorrow would be a brand new day, for him.

Chapter Twenty Four

It had been ten days since Drew had been killed. Denny and Caroline were back in the Barker house on Chena Ridge, having returned from Drew's memorial, which was held in Salcha.

After the ceremony, Charlie Brady had held a small reception at the diner, with finger foods and drinks. Besides Charlie, Caroline, and Denny, there were sixteen other people who had known Drew. He'd had no family other than his grandfather.

Charlie found a moment to talk privately with Denny. "Do you have any idea who could have done this, Denny?"

Denny was silent for a moment, before saying, "No, Charlie."

But Brady knew Denny well and wasn't buying it.

"You know you can talk to me, right? Anything you tell me won't go any further unless you want it to. So, again, I ask you, who do you think did this?"

Denny knew Charlie was as trustworthy a man as he could have for a friend. But, how much could he tell him, without spoiling his chances to make things right? Brady had been a trooper for a long time, after all. Finally Caraway made his decision.

"Charlie, do you believe there are times, situations, when something usually considered to be wrong is the right thing to do?"

Charlie knew exactly what Denny was suggesting. He stood for a moment, looking at a man he knew was capable of dealing with almost anything, including this. "You're my good friend, Caraway, and I wouldn't want you to pay the price for taking it on yourself to right an obvious wrong, but yes, I do believe what you asked is true. So, talk to me."

"Before Drew died, he spoke two words to me: 'Red beard'."

For a moment what Denny said didn't register, until the significance of those two words hit home. All Charlie said was, "Damn."

"And I'll tell you this, Charlie, that bullet was meant for me. I know it."

Caroline came over, saw the looks the two men were giving each other, then turned and walked away, saying, "I don't want to know."

Charlie asked Denny if he was going out to the homestead. Denny told him he would, once Caroline was back at home.

"Give me a little time. I'll make a few general inquiries. I still have friends on the force, so maybe I'll have something once you come back in, as I know you will. But, no promises."

The two friends shook hands then went back to the others, who were eating, drinking, talking about Drew, and telling stories about their friend. One of the guys who had known him well, a long-time Salcha resident, after several shots of bourbon, began singing Danny Boy. He didn't have the best voice, but the emotion behind it quieted every one down. It was a strong, bittersweet moment.

Back in Fairbanks, sitting in the living room, Denny and Caroline talked quietly, over coffee. He would return to his homestead in a few days. Caroline had asked if he really thought he'd be up for continuing to run the lodge, after what had happened. "You know I'm happy to be there with you Denny, but, I'd understand if you wanted to let go of it now."

"I've given it some thought, Caroline, and as bad as things are right now, I don't plan to give it up, at least not for the foreseeable future. I've got to make a living, and I can't think of a better way to do it. I do love the lodge. Your father had a real gift for getting things right, and Burl Lake is one of them. You know I have a lot of respect and love for him, and keeping the lodge going makes me feel I'm honoring his memory. It's great having you and Max there with me, too."

Chapter Twenty Five

Winter, this time around, was running colder than it had for the past several years. Denny was glad he had built up a good supply of firewood for the homestead. There had been several heavy snow storms already, and it was barely January.

If the weather had been milder, he would have already gone into Salcha to find out if Charlie had learned anything. He'd prefer to do that, rather than talking over the VHF radio. But, the land was deeply covered with snow. The paths Denny had cleared around the homestead resembled tunnels, the piled-up snow almost over his head. He was glad he'd put in a high opening window on the back wall of the cabin. If this kept up, he might have to use it to leave the cabin. Alaska was definitely flexing its muscles this winter.

Rip hung around the cabin, the heavy snow more than he wanted to deal with, except when he had to take care of natural business, after which he wanted right back in.

But Denny worked through it, as he had managed all the past situations he'd been confronted with while living remote. His perishable foods were almost gone, but he had managed to ration his potatoes, butter, coffee, and sugar. In a week, maybe two, he'd be all out. But he had taken a good moose late in the fall, so he had meat.

At the end of February, a call came in on his VHF radio. It was Charlie Brady.

"I was mainly calling to see how you've been faring this winter. I know it must be really heavy out your way; it's deep here. I have your truck here at my place, safe and sound, but the roof of the old trailer caved in under the snow load after the last storm. Sorry, Denny."

"It was an old unit and bound to go bad sometime, Charlie, so don't worry, I'll manage."

"Well, I have an offer to make you, Denny, about Drew's place, the one his grandfather left him. I bought the house at the state auction held for the property; structures and everything there. It was sold as is, lock, stock, and barrel. Turned out there was only one other bidder, and he thought he could get it for nothing. I didn't pay much for it myself. Anyway, I'll be staying there instead of the little cabin at the cafe, so that's available. Anyway, we'll talk after you come in."

"Okay Charlie. Listen, have you found out anything yet?"

"Nothing. The man seems to have fallen off the map. Nobody knows anything. His buddy, the pilot who used to work for him, supposedly doesn't know where he is either, or so he says. I told a friend at the office I was curious about an old case Red Beard was involved in, to tie up some loose ends on a charge leveled at him, which he'd been able to slip out of. Denny, I don't know what else to tell you right now."

"I appreciate all your help Charlie, but I'd feel better if you'd let it go at this point. I don't want you to get any more involved than you already are. Besides, I'm not sure if I'm going to pursue it any more myself. I'll see you as soon as I get the trail broken. I'm running out of coffee."

After Charlie signed off, Denny sat by the wood stove, sipping a cup of tea. He disliked lying to his friend, but he wanted to keep him out of harm's way, in case his plan went bad.

Denny knew where O'Bannion was. If he told anyone how, Denny figured they'd give him a funny look, thinking he had gone bushy for sure.

Three days before Charlie called him, Denny had a dream. He didn't dream much, but when he did it was often a message, and very real, as in the dreams he'd had of his grandfather, which told him his granddad was watching over him.

Denny had dreamed of the white caribou again. This time, the bull was standing next to a very familiar shack, pawing the ground in front of the door.

The little structure was the first hunting shack he had built while working for O'Bannion. He woke up knowing O'Bannion was holed up there. He didn't know if the man would leave before winter was over or not, so Denny decided to heed the unusual message and travel out to the remote area where the shack was. It would be a rough go. He was sure the snowfall would be heavy in the country he had already traveled through on foot, when O'Bannion had marooned him there, years before.

Denny took two skis off his big freighter sled, and rigged them up on the smaller, lighter, plastic-bodied trailer he usually towed behind his ATV, in place of the wheels normally mounted there. He had been able to use some of the support pieces from the big sled to brace them. Done with the modifications, Caraway figured it would hold up. He needed the smaller, lighter sled to carry extra fuel for his snow machine, as well as all his trail gear, on this trip.

Five days after Charlie's call, Denny was set to go north. He had spent two full days opening up the worst places on the trail.

Denny was concerned about his dog, but Rip had stayed in the cabin, patiently waiting. When Denny had returned after the first day of trail breaking, Rip was overcome with seeing him again, jumping on him, barking, and whining. The dog ran outside to deal with what he had held in all day, not wanting to soil his home.

On the second morning, after he told the dog to stay, Rip was upset. He went over to the little rug and lay down, his face turned away from Caraway. Denny quietly but firmly called him, and the dog turned his head to look at him.

Leaving a goodly portion of moose meat in Rip's dish, he said, "I'll be back later, boy."

Rip laid his head down on the rug again and blew out a breath, rippling his jowls. Denny, knowing the meaning behind the act, couldn't help smiling.

The second day of trail breaking was worse. Denny got bogged down a half dozen times, and he'd had to break trail with snowshoes, after digging out the front of the snow machine. As he had many times in the past, Caraway got the job done, leaving off about a mile from the highway. Some snow machine riders had already carved some trails there, saving Denny a little extra work. Barring any additional snow fall, he would be okay.

When he got home, very late and exhausted, he was greeted by a very unhappy dog. Walking into the cabin, he stepped in something soft and immediately knew what it was.

Denny found and flipped on the electric light over the table, before taking off the offending boot. Rip was standing on his rug, giving Denny an accusing look. Denny opened the door again, and Rip walked out, stiff legged. Denny cleaned up the mess by the door and off his boot.

He let the dog back in when he scratched on the door. Rip tried to ignore Denny, but the homesteader began rubbing his head and scratching his ribs, talking quietly to the dog, apologizing for leaving him alone, until Rip gave him a little forgiving lick on the hand and leaned against Caraway, signifying everything was all right.

The next day, Denny Caraway was on the trail to Salcha. The temperature had risen a few degrees, but the snow stayed firm, making the ride a little easier.

Denny had gotten Rip to sit on the back portion of the snow machine seat. A mile down the trail, he had jumped off once to run, but after finding out the hard way how deep the snow was, he gladly climbed back on the seat and remained there.

In Salcha, Denny had to check in with Charlie to get his truck for the ride north.

Brady was happy to see Denny and poured him a cup of coffee, made his favorite meal of a burger and fries, and gave Rip a piece of ground beef behind the counter. He stood talking to Caraway, and it didn't take him long to realize Denny was still planning to find and deal with Drew's murderer, but Brady said nothing.

Brady again told Denny he was going to be living in Elliot's place now, instead of the little cabin behind the cafe, and Caraway was welcome to stay in the cabin any time he came into Salcha. Brady was going to offer Caraway a room at Elliot's old house, since there was enough space there, but he knew Denny would prefer a place of his own to stay in while in Salcha. "I hope you'll be willing to use the cabin, Denny, when you come into town in the future. There's plenty of room for you to leave your rigs there too, of course."

"I'll do that Charlie, no worries."

"Make sure you do. I seem to be losing friends more and more as life rolls on. I'd be happy if you outlived me."

"Charlie, I'm going to take a snow machine ride for a few days and explore some country I haven't seen in winter before. Think you could watch Rip for awhile? He's a good dog and shouldn't be any trouble."

"Sure, Denny, he'll be all right with me. If I have any trouble with customers, he can be my backup."

Caraway was going to hand Charlie some money for the meal, but Brady raised his hand. Standing and zipping up his parka, Denny nodded. "I don't plan on disappearing again, no matter what. You take care, my friend."

Caraway went out to his truck and started it warming. He noticed the gas tank was full and smiled to himself.

He pulled out the ramps, unhitched the sled, and rode the snow machine up into the truck's eight-foot bed. Unloading the little improvised snow machine sled, he put the gear and supplies in the cab and stashed the empty trailer in the bed, also. Backing out from the North Star Cafe, he pulled onto the road and headed north.

Chapter Twenty Six

Denny reached the place where he intended to park the truck while he was making his run. It was an extra wide pull-out, where the truck could sit for a while without raising any suspicions from a passing trooper. People were always parking off the side of Alaskan roads while they took snow machine rides, or other little adventures.

He sat for a while studying a map of the game management unit where he had built the hunting camp. He had a good idea where he had to go, but winter would make it a very different place to travel through, compared to the last time he had been there, walking out in summer. It would also be a much faster journey, when available light allowed.

It had been a few years since he'd been there, but because of the circumstances, the terrain he traveled over had been imprinted in his mind. Denny could decipher the changes winter would make of the territory. He figured he'd need to stay out several nights and could probably make it to his destination by the afternoon of the third day. Only making the ride would tell what it would really take to get there.

Denny was using his instincts and experience in the wilderness to guide him as much as his map and compass. Snow and winds had altered some areas. Twice, he'd needed to backtrack a few miles to get his bearings, but he knew he was heading in the right general direction.

Caraway was surprised and relieved that the snow wasn't more difficult to travel over. He had expected some rough places that would hold him back. But, except for two areas where the deep snow required breaking some short stretches of trail on snowshoes and digging out the bogged down machine, it all went easily. Denny decided it was probably because he was doing the right thing, though he knew, deep down, he was just lucky the snow wasn't worse.

It was less difficult for Caraway, making the journey to the hunting shack in winter. If he'd had to come out by wheeler in summer, it may well have been worse than going it on foot, especially through the swampy areas he remembered. In winter, all the streams and bogs he'd had to deal with were hard frozen and no longer obstacles. He wished it was a casual ride to explore the country and enjoy some winter camping, but such was not the case. Still, his resolve was strong.

As he rode, staying alert and observing where he was, memories from the past ran through his mind. He remembered special moments he'd had with Gwen and with Nathan, Caroline, and even little Max. He had to shake his head and clear his mind at times, to concentrate on the trail.

As soon as all available light went away, Denny found a good place to camp for the night. He dug out a shelter in the snow, covered most of the opening with an emergency foil blanket, placing another under him, and got as comfortable as possible. The down sleeping bag kept him warm enough to allow some sleep, a necessity for staying focused and not slipping up somewhere along the trail.

The second night out, he heard wolves howling, and the sounds were growing closer, close enough to make him slip out of his bag and stand watching in the freezing night air with his headlamp on.

Minutes later, visible in the beam of light, were four wolves, only a few yards away, their eyes reflecting eerily as they moved their heads about, testing the air. Denny stood quietly, pistol in hand.

The wolves, their curiosity satisfied after identifying the intruder in their territory, melted back into the darkness.

After waiting to make sure they were really gone, Caraway slipped back into his bag, but he was only half asleep the rest of the night, his pistol staying warm inside the bag, within easy reach.

As he had figured, early in the afternoon of the third day, he spotted the hunting shack about two hundred yards away. Denny ran the snow machine up to a snowy mound and shut it down.

Lying so only his head was visible, Denny pulled a small pair of binoculars from his parka pocket to watch the hunting shack he had built years ago. Building it had been a good time for him, aside from O'Bannion and the fool of a client he had taken on the brown bear hunt. He had enjoyed being out on his own in this wild country for the first time.

There was no smoke coming from the shack's stovepipe, but Denny could see the snow had been cleared away from the area around the front door. Denny spotted half-buried caribou bones and antlers at the corner of the shack. What appeared to be a snow-covered ATV was parked by the side wall.

After watching for half an hour, he moved up closer to the small structure, his rifle now in hand. Denny crouched in the snow, staying out of sight. There was no one at the shack, so Caraway took a chance and slipped in through the unlocked door, banging his boots together first to get rid of any loose snow.

Inside, the place was a mess. Empty food cans had been tossed in one corner, along with other food packaging. There were pieces of rabbit skin and feathers as well, probably ptarmigan. There were dirty dishes on the counter and a slop bucket partially filled with greasy, half-frozen water on the floor. The sheepherder's stove was still slightly warm, but the uninsulated shack was cold.

Going back outside, Denny stood looking around, wondering where the person staying in the shack had gone.

Walking to the side of the shack facing the small lake, Denny saw some snow-shoe tracks heading up and over the little rise between the building and the lake. He had put on his bear paw snowshoes before he left the snow machine, removing them before entering the shack. Now, he put them back on.

Caraway began following the trail of disturbed snow, staying as low as he could. Available light was already minimal, but Denny continued on, keeping his snowshoes in the prints O'Bannion had made, if they actually were his.

Denny had just topped the little rise, when he saw someone out on the frozen lake beyond. He dropped down into a prone position to watch. The man on the lake had his back to Denny, wearing a parka with the hood up. He appeared to be ice fishing.

After about ten minutes, the man stood up, turned around, and began walking back towards the shack. Denny prepared himself for what was to come. But with darkness nearly complete, the man walked right past where Denny lay half buried in snow, without seeing him. He had an axe, probably for cutting a hole in the ice, and two fish on a stringer in his left hand.

The man stopped and looked to the right and left, turning partway around as he did. Denny caught a brief glimpse of a heavy beard, and knew who it was.

O'Bannion remained standing there, listening and looking for anything to be wary of. He might have been a miserable human being, but he was also an experienced outdoorsman, no stranger to the wilderness. Something had made him edgy. Denny held his breath and waited, rifle already cocked.

The old guide continued walking to the hut and went in. A moment later, the light of a lantern lit up the snow outside the shack's one window, on the back wall.

Denny stood up, took off his snowshoes, and crept to the shack. But he waited before he made his next move, to let O'Bannion settle down. He stood listening and waiting.

Denny moved close to the door, set his rifle carefully against the wooden wall, and took out his pistol. He slowly cocked it to keep sound to a minimum, reached out his hand, and began to turn the door knob.

It felt as if someone very powerful had punched him in the side, at the same moment a loud BOOM! sounded inside the shack. A small piece of the door had blown out, hitting Caraway with bits of wooden shrapnel.

Denny fell flat on his back, but managed to roll over onto his left side, the side the bullet had passed through. He lay perfectly still, fighting to stay conscious, trying to keep from breathing deeply or making any noise, despite the searing pain.

The door slowly opened, casting light from the lantern inside onto the scene outside. O'Bannion, his parka hood down, stepped out, .357 magnum in hand. He saw the rifle standing against the wall and made a scoffing noise.

"Left your rifle standing there, damn fool." Carlton spoke out loud, thinking Caraway was dead from the round he had fired through the door.

"Thought you were pretty clever, did you, finding me out here? Well, you're not the only smart old bull in the woods!"

O'Bannion gave Denny a hard kick in the back. Somehow, Caraway managed to take it, not giving himself away. Watching Denny for any signs of life, O'Bannion walked around, and putting his boot against Caraway's right arm, pushed to roll him onto his back.

The moment Denny felt the boot against his arm, he was ready. As he rolled over, he brought the pistol out and up, firing without hesitation. O'Bannion was flung backwards in reaction to the shot, slamming onto the snow.

Denny managed to sit up, the pistol still pointing at his fatally wounded foe. He got to his knees and made his way over to O'Bannion's twitching body. The man wasn't quite dead yet. O'Bannion coughed, blood flowing out of his mouth. He looked at Denny and tried to say something, but couldn't speak.

His eyes showing no pity for the dying man in front of him, Caraway said, "That was for Drew."

O'Bannion's eyes widened, and his face twisted in a grotesque grimace. He reached out a hand and tried to grab the front of Caraway's parka, but couldn't. His arm dropped back down, and Carlton O'Bannion was no more.

Somehow, Caraway managed to do all he needed to, before collapsing onto the bunk, weak and in great pain. He had gone into the little frame shack after retrieving the first aid kit and sleeping bag from the sled. The long walk to and from the snow machine had been rough.

By lantern light, after restarting the fire in the stove from the small stack of firewood inside, he managed to inspect and do what he could to clean and dress the entry wound. The exit wound in his back was larger, but he couldn't reach it easily. Still, he managed to put a double patch of gauze bandage on it, taping it in place. Too weak to do more, he would move O'Bannion's body in the morning and conceal it somewhere out on the tundra. But for now, he needed to rest. He passed out as soon as he lay down on the bunk.

It was light when Denny awoke. He sat up with difficulty, feeling very stiff, and grunted from the harsh stab of pain as he managed to stand.

He changed the gauze pads on both wounds and saw there hadn't been much bleeding. Caraway knew he was very lucky, realizing the bullet had punched through him without hitting any vital organs or major arteries. Still, it had done enough damage to put him in a bad way.

Hungry, he opened his pack to find and eat a piece of jerky and some fry bread, with a cup of tea he made over the little wood stove. Denny slowly put on his parka and went outside to deal with O'Bannion's remains.

Denny Caraway had seen a lot of things over the years he had lived in the wilds, but what he saw in front of the cabin was difficult to handle, even for him. Wolves had come in the night and taken care of the dead man lying there. There appeared to have been at least five or six of them. It hadn't taken long for the animals to devour the remains, leaving little behind.

Caraway went back inside the shack to gather up his pack and guns, glad to leave the grisly scene. He made sure there was nothing connecting him to the situation and made his way through the snow back to his machine.

Pulling the starter cord sent a searing pain through his middle, but luckily, even in the icy morning air, it started up after only a few yanks. Making a wide swing around, he began backtracking on the trail he had come in on, leaving what was left of O'Bannion to the elements.

Chapter Twenty Seven

Denny rode at a steady pace, but held his speed down to lessen the jolts and bounces of the trail, trying to minimize the pain.

He continued on even after dark. Because there had been no snowfall since he had come in, his trail was easy to follow by headlight. He was concerned his tracks might be followed by some others on snow machines or perhaps in a snow cat, but there was nothing he could do about it. Caraway had to get some help soon. The blood loss and tissue damage he had sustained had weakened him, and infection was inevitable. There was only once place he could think of where he might be taken care of without arousing suspicion.

Denny had to camp for one night, too weak to continue on without resting. He dug a shallow trench with his hands, laid an emergency blanket down for a ground cover, and worked himself into the sleeping bag. He was hungry, but too tired to do anything about it. Denny was out the moment he lay down.

Caraway woke up with several inches of snow covering him. A light, steady snowfall was coming down.

Forcing himself up, he crammed his sleeping bag into the sled, cleared the snow from the snow machine, got it going with some difficulty, and rode on towards the highway. The tracks from his ride in were barely visible, but Denny was closer to the road than he thought. After several more hours of riding, stopping once to pour the last of the extra fuel into the tank and adding engine oil, Denny made it to the highway. It took some searching to find his truck. Luckily, he tried heading north first, and found it about a mile from where he had come out onto the highway.

Denny ran the snow machine up the ramps into the bed of the truck, loaded the gear from the little trailer into the cab, and managed to shove the trailer in next to the snow machine. He'd had to stop many times to gather what strength he had left. Climbing into the cab, he sat shivering more from the exertion and pain than the cold, until his body settled down, and the pain had subsided.

Denny was feverish, his mind foggy, but he managed to get the truck started and drove to Fairbanks. There was no way he could make it to Salcha and on to his homestead, and even if he managed to make it out to his cabin, he wouldn't last long. Though he didn't want to get Caroline involved, Denny had no choice. He didn't plan on going under, not because of O'Bannion.

Caraway must have had an angel on his shoulder. Slipping in and out of consciousness as he drove, it was only by pure good fortune he didn't run off the road into the trees or down an embankment.

Caroline was busy with Max in the Barker house when she heard a vehicle horn go off in front.

She opened the front door and saw Everett Tanner at Denny's truck. He had the cab door open, helping Denny out. Caroline came running to help.

The two of them got Denny into a bedroom. They took off his boots, parka, and shirt. Already upset by the large blood stains and the holes in the shirt, after they took it off, Caroline gasped to see the gauze patches crusted with dried blood. Tanner carefully peeled them off. Some clotted blood came with them.

"Miss Barker, he's been shot. Looks like it went right through. I better call an ambulance; it appears infection's already set in."

Denny grabbed Everett's arm and said, "No ambulance! No hospital! You have to do it. Please."

Denny's eyes rolled back, and he passed out.

Tanner and Caroline looked at each other, great concern in Caroline's eyes.

After thinking it over, Tanner said, "I was a medic in the army. I still remember some things about wounds, but it's been a long time. We need antibiotics and something to clean out the wounds."

Caroline went to the bathroom and brought out antibiotic cream and some tablets she had from a previous illness.

"I don't know if these are the right kind, but they're all I have."

"At least it's something," he said.

Tanner worked on Denny as well as he could. There was fabric from the parka and some small wood splinters from the shack door in the wound. It was fortunate Denny was unconscious, because a lot of prodding and probing was necessary to clean the wounds. Tanner coated them with antibiotic cream after cleaning out the dead tissue from the edges. He used an

X-Acto knife with a rounded blade which Caroline had found in her father's desk. Everett sterilized it with heat from the kitchen stove. It wasn't a scalpel, but it worked well enough.

Using fine fishing monofilament with a curved sewing needle Caroline provided, he did a reasonable job of suturing the wounds, leaving a little strip of rolled gauze hanging out of them both, for drainage.

"It's all we can do for now," Tanner said. "If he gets worse, he'll have to go to the hospital, without a doubt."

"Mr. Tanner, Everett," Caroline said, "I don't know how or why this happened to Denny, but I know him very well. Whatever the situation, I'm sure he wasn't at fault. He's a good man, so please, let's try to help him ourselves, as he asked."

"Miss Barker, I've worked on jobs a number of times where Mr. Caraway was our protection in the wilderness. I know he would have risked his life for us. He saved us from a bad bear on Kodiak, so I agree he's a good man. I really think a hospital would be best, but we'll do as he wishes. Let's give it a few days and see how it goes. Whatever the reason he got shot must have been unavoidable, I'm sure."

Caroline nodded, and Tanner, after cleaning up the bloody mess, left her to sit with Denny. Max played on the floor at her feet, oblivious to the serious situation.

Caraway slept for a full twenty-four hours. He had a high fever and kept mumbling in his sleep. Caroline kept him cooled off with a damp washcloth, waking him to take antibiotic pills.

The next afternoon, Caroline woke up from a nap on the couch. Max had been sleeping with her, but he was gone. She heard a whispery voice calling her.

She ran into Denny's room to find Max lying next to Denny, patting him on the chest.

"Den, mommy!" he said, with a concerned look on his face.

Caroline picked him up and told her son everything was okay, and that Denny was only sleepy.

"I'm thirsty, C," Caraway whispered.

Caroline went to the kitchen and poured Denny a glass of orange juice. She knew it would be good for him. He drank it down quickly and asked for more, finished the second glass too, before falling asleep again, after saying, "Glad to be home." Caroline's heart ached to see Caraway in such a state, as she sat keeping watch over him.

Denny was in and out for several days, but the fever broke on the morning of the third day, and he was able to eat some soup Caroline had made. She wanted to ask him what had happened, but held her tongue, waiting for him to tell her.

Two days later, Denny came slowly shuffling out to the living room. Caroline and Max were sitting on the couch reading a book.

"I sure am hungry," Denny said in a rough voice. "Have anything for lunch, like maybe a burger?"

Caroline smiled and told Denny, "Actually, some soup would probably be better for now, but I'll make you a grilled cheese sandwich."

Putting some soup on to warm, Caroline sat Denny down and changed his dressings. Denny winced as she pulled off the taped-on gauze pads.

"Your wounds are looking much better, Denny. The infection seems to be gone, and there's no drainage. Looks like you got lucky."

Caroline explained what had happened after he'd passed out and how Tanner had treated him.

There was a knock at the door, and Caroline let Everett Tanner in. It was the first time Caraway had actually seen him since he had passed out on the bed.

"I'm glad to see you up and about, Mr. Caraway. Feeling better?"

"Much better. Thanks, Tanner. I'm grateful for what you've done. I hope it will set well with you if we just let the situation fade away and you'd accept my word there was no wrong-doing on my part. It would be best for me if this was forgotten. If there's ever anything I can do for you, I want you to let me know."

Looking at Denny directly, Everett said, "Consider it done, and we're good."

Caroline brought Denny the soup and sandwich, which Caraway devoured.

Caraway spent the rest of the winter and into the spring recovering at Caroline's house. Though he was healing from the wound itself, he needed time to rebuild his strength and health.

Charlie Brady had called several times to see if Caroline had heard from Caraway, and she had finally told him what was going on. She knew he and Denny were best friends and decided to trust the man.

One morning, Charlie Brady showed up at the Barker house. He had to see Denny for himself to satisfy his concerns. Caroline left the two friends to talk.

"Looks like you survived, Denny. Did anyone else?"

"Not to my knowledge, Charlie. Have there been any reports of depredation by animals on humans out west of Fairbanks, north of McGrath?"

"Nothing I've heard about, and I've been checking for anything unusual, regularly. Why?"

"Let's say wolves don't leave behind much of anything they find for food."

Brady stared at Denny for a few seconds and shook his head. "So, any concerns over Drew's murder can be laid to rest, at least between us?"

"Yes, Charlie, it's done."

The two men continued talking about other things, the subject of Denny's latest adventure being closed.

Charlie got up to leave and told Denny he had brought someone to see him. They went out to the front porch. Max and Rip were playing there. Rip saw Denny, let out an excited cry, and ran to Caraway, almost knocking him over in his joy and excitement.

"He's gotten a little chubby, Charlie, but he looks good. Thanks."

"A dog having a little extra weight up here isn't so bad, Denny. I'm going to miss the mutt."

Brady took his leave, telling Denny how glad he was things had worked out, for both of them. Sitting in his truck, he said, "You know, if it hadn't gone well for you, I wouldn't have had any choice but to step in, and I'm not talking about telling anyone else about it."

"I know, Charlie. I'm glad it wasn't necessary."

One night, unable to keep it in any longer, Caroline, over dinner, asked Denny what had happened.

"C, the less I tell you, the better I'd feel. If you don't know, you're not involved, okay? But I will say one thing: Drew's murder has been repaid. That's all you need to know."

Caroline read the expression on Caraway's face, nodded, and never brought it up again.

For his part, Tanner was a man of his word. He never spoke of the incident to anyone. Everett remembered Caraway walking into the tall grass on Kodiak to sniff out the bad bear. He figured Denny was equal parts the bravest and craziest man he knew, and he had great respect for him.

Denny was sitting at Nathan's desk in early May, Rip lying at his feet under the desk. He was going over the reservations Caroline had made, at his insistence. He had no intention of letting the next season at Burl Lake Lodge be interrupted. He was feeling generally fit again, other than having occasional moments of weakness. Though the wounds themselves had healed, a person can't go through such trauma without some after effects, even Denny Caraway. It had been a shock to his body. Ever after, he suffered from random aches and pains in the part of his body where he had been shot.

Caroline came in with a cup of coffee and asked him what he thought about the clients she had booked.

"They look fine, C. I'm glad to see several of the people are repeat customers, including Marcel Durier."

"Me too. I'm glad Robert Pete has agreed to be our assistant fishing guide. He seems a solid guy, and I love his wife Evie. She knows how to cook all sorts of Alaskan-style food, and with her constant bright smile, she'll be a welcome addition to the lodge, as well."

"If I hadn't agreed to hire her too, Robert wouldn't have accepted. Besides, I wanted someone there to help you with chores at the lodge."

"What about Lanyard Creek, Denny? Will you need to go out there to check on things?"

"I'd like to go after spring break-up to see how the place is holding up. Robert has suggested going out with me, but I'm sure I'll be fine."

"Okay. Will you be out there long?"

"Only long enough to check the place out and spend the night, then I'll be back."

"Good, I wouldn't want you to be gone too long."

"Why, C, are you worried about this worn-out old homesteader?"

"No, Denny," Caroline said, "I'd worry about you, the toughest and best man I know." She added, "Besides my daddy, of course."

Caraway smiled. "Of course. Let's have a drink to celebrate a new and hopefully great season at the lake."

Chapter Twenty Eight

Denny Caraway sat waiting on the dock, two rods and reels lying next to him, and Rip lying on the dock behind him. He wondered where the six-year-old boy he was waiting for had gone off to. Max knew he didn't like to be kept waiting when fishing was concerned.

Rapid little footsteps sounded on the dock planking, and Rip jumped up to greet his young friend.

"Sorry, Denny, momma said I had to finish my chores before I came out."

"Well, I can't find fault there. Let's get our lines in the water."

The old man and the young boy sat side by side, waiting for a bite. It had become a ritual. Once the season was over and the clients were all gone, they spent some time every afternoon fishing for themselves.

Burl Lake had been good to them. The lodge had become a success from the very start, and it appeared it would remain so.

Max finally spoke: "Den, do you miss your home out in the woods when you're here at the lodge?"

Caraway thought for a moment. "Well, I do stay there in the winter," he said, tickling the boy's ribs, making him squirm. "Though, if I was always there, I'd miss you a lot."

"I'm happy you stay with us at the house sometimes. I know mom's glad, too."

Caroline came out with some iced tea for the boys. She sat down with Max between herself and Denny.

"I expected to see a half-dozen nice trout on the stringer by now. What's the problem?"

Max beamed up at her, "Sure mom, whatever you say."

The boy set the rod down and put his little arms around the two people he loved most. Caroline put her arm behind the boy, her hand resting on Denny's back.

"Denny," Caroline said, "couldn't we stay on a few more days? There's no hurry, is there?"

"Nope, C, there isn't. I'm in no hurry to leave. Max and I can get some more fishing in."

Caroline sat staring out over the lake, a tiny sigh escaping from her lips. If Caraway noticed it, he said nothing.

The three of them sat quietly on the dock, a few feet off the shore of Burl Lake, beauty all around them.

Truth to tell, not one of them really cared if the fish were biting or not.

Chapter Twenty Nine

They had just returned to Fairbanks from Burl Lake, when the phone rang at the Barker house. Tanner and Denny were unloading the Suburban, and Maxwell was running around, playing with Rip. Because Caroline was spending every summer at Burl Lake, she had hired Tanner to be at the house full time. He took care of everything and had no complaints about the work.

Caroline had answered the phone and was talking seriously in a low voice. Denny got a funny feeling, seeing the way she was acting.

"Fine," Caroline said, "but, you needn't have any expectations."

She hung up and stood there, deep in thought.

Denny walked over to ask her if everything was okay. She looked disturbed and confused.

"Denny, that call was from Chad. He wants to come over and talk."

"And is he coming over?"

"Yes, though I don't know why. He has no reason to expect anything to come of it."

"Are you sure, Caroline?"

"Well, he is Max's father, biologically."

Denny nodded and walked away to help Tanner finish unloading. He didn't allow himself to worry about the call and what it might mean. In several days he'd be going out to the homestead.

The next day, Denny was in his room getting all his things together for the trail ride out to the creek.

He left the bedroom, hearing loud voices. Standing in the hall, he saw Caroline at the door with a man he figured was Chad, her former fiancé and Max's absentee father. Denny had only met him once, briefly, years ago.

Walking up, he glared at Chad, and asked Caroline if everything was okay. Chad, for his part, glared back at Caraway, seeing he was in the house.

She told Denny it was all right and to please give them some time to talk. Still staring at Chad, he nodded and went out to the back yard where Tanner was busy fixing the fence, while Max played with a toy truck. Rip was sniffing at something under a tree.

Denny stood looking at the domestic scene all around him, and it suddenly hit him, giving him a chill. He was doing it again, straying from the path that destiny had set for him.

Though he hadn't said anything to her yet, Denny had decided to be with Caroline, completely. He cared deeply for her and Max, so it made sense to him, until now. He had planned to tell her before he left, to give her time to decide.

But, everything had changed. The call from Chad had been a strong signal to him.

Caraway knew, deep in his heart, he had to go home to Lanyard Creek to live alone as he should, as a remote homesteader. He had only spent winters there over the past several years. Caraway knew he missed it more than he was willing to admit. The thought that he might put Caroline and Max in harm's way, as he believed he had done with Gwen, was too much for him to consider. Once more, Denny Caraway had to do what was necessary.

Caroline came out a while later, a conflicted look on her face. Denny smiled a tight little smile, saying, "He wants to try and make things right, doesn't he? He's Max's father and you realize you still have feelings for him, so you're going to give it a go, right?"

Caroline's face went sad, and she hung her head, not wanting to look into Caraway's eyes. "I do love you, Denny."

"And I love you too, Caroline, but there's a lot going on here, including and especially about Max."

"But how can things stay the same between us and at Burl Lake?"

"They can't, C. You have to decide what is most important to you. No matter what, you and I will be okay. I'm going back to the homestead tomorrow, and I'll return in a few weeks to see how things are. I don't want you to worry about me." Denny leaned forward and kissed Caroline on the cheek.

He went back to his room and sat on the edge of the bed. Rip came up to him and put his muzzle against Denny's hand. Caraway hadn't told Caroline about the realization he'd had, knowing it would have disturbed her. He also knew if she and Chad could make a go of it, it would probably be for the best.

Denny petted his dog and said, "We're going home tomorrow, boy, we're going home."

Epilogue

D enny Caraway looked up from the moose he was field dressing. It would be his meat for the winter. He stood for a moment, letting his achy back relax, before finishing the task at hand.

His mind wandered back several years, to the last time he had been to Burl Lake Fishing Lodge. It had been a good season.

He no longer owned the lodge, having sold it to Caroline Barker, after her decision to let her former fiancé, Chad Merritt, back into her life. Caraway had returned to his homestead full time. The amount of money she gave him for the lodge was enough to sustain him for many years, living the simple life of a remote homesteader.

She had told him that any time he wanted to manage the lodge for her, it would be fine, but he knew that wouldn't happen. He believed his remote home was the only place his life could be as it should, on the proper path for him to follow.

Caraway was never lonely there, having the forest and its inhabitants all around him. His dog Rip also kept him company, sharing his journeys out from the cabin, to hunt, fish, and enjoy their wilderness home. Rip had grown into a great bush dog, tough and fearless, but obedient to Denny's every command.

There was one black bear who learned it was best to avoid the homestead. One morning, it had come to eat the vegetables Denny had growing in his new garden, until Rip had rushed the animal, nipping at his flanks, avoiding the bear's claws and teeth, until the bruin had given up in frustration and run off, much to Caraway's enjoyment and relief.

Rip was getting old, however, and Denny knew he would lose his friend eventually. So, he would go to Robert Pete's home soon and get another pup to raise. Rip would enjoy having a young dog around, also.

He also had his friend Charlie Brady to visit in Salcha, during the occasional times he went into town. Denny had taken to buying his perishable foods from Charlie, avoiding the need to go into Fairbanks. Brady had decided to have a two pump gas island installed next to the North Star. It would be good for the locals, as well as road travelers.

Brady, for his part, had visited the homestead several times and would again. They enjoyed spending time together, sometimes teasing each other about their growing list of aches and pains.

Caroline and Chad were now a solid couple, having squared things away as Denny had known they would, and the three of them, including Max, were a nice little family. Caraway would visit for Thanksgiving, along with Charlie Brady, but not Christmas, which he would spend on the homestead alone, with his beloved wife, Gwen, nearby.

Caraway had no regrets. He had come to accept everything in his life as what was meant to be.

But one thing the woodsman knew for sure: he was where he belonged, a solitary man deep in the Alaska wilderness, living the best life he'd ever known.

Finis

8443866R00087

Made in the USA
San Bernardino, CA
10 February 2014